This book
belongs to

....

First published in 2018 by Miles Kelly Publishing Ltd
Harding's Barn, Bardfield End Green, Thaxted, Essex, CM6 3PX, UK

2 4 6 8 10 9 7 5 3 1

Publishing Director Belinda Gallagher
Creative Director Jo Cowan
Editorial Director Rosie Neave
Senior Editor Becky Miles
Design Managers Joe Jones, Simon Lee
Image Manager Liberty Newton
Production Elizabeth Collins, Caroline Kelly
Reprographics Stephan Davis, Jennifer Cozens
Assets Lorraine King

ISBN 978-1-78617-478-9

Printed in China

British Library Cataloguing-in-Publication Data
A catalogue record for this book is available from the British Library

Acknowledgements

The publishers would like to thank the following artists who have contributed to this book:
Advocate Art: Natalia Moore
The Bright Agency: Maddie Frost (decorative frames), Maxine Lee

Made with paper from a sustainable forest

www.mileskelly.net

The Story of Princess Haya

The Twelve Brothers

MILES KELLY

The Story of Princess Haya

When Princess Haya was little, her mother died and her father remarried. His new wife was mean to Princess Haya saying, "You are not my child!" But Haya was a good

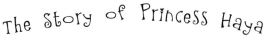

and kind young girl.
One day the Emperor of
Japan visited Princess Haya's
home. He asked Haya and
her stepmother to play him
some music. Princess Haya
had worked hard learning
her music, but her
stepmother
was lazy
and hadn't
practised

much. Haya played beautifully, but her stepmother kept forgetting the notes. The Emperor was not pleased with the stepmother, but he gave Haya gifts for playing so well.

This made the stepmother angry. She wanted to get rid of Haya, so she bought some poison. Then she carefully poured two glasses of orange juice, one for her son and one for Haya. She put the poison in one glass. However, she muddled up the glasses and gave the poisoned drink to her son by mistake. Suddenly the boy screamed and dropped to the floor. The stepmother blamed Haya for this and disliked her even more.

When Princess Haya was thirteen, her beautiful singing was spoken about across the land. At this time it rained so much that many of the fields were flooded. The Emperor hated hearing the drumming sound of the rain and became ill with worry. He asked Princess Haya to sing for him at his palace to make him feel better.

So Haya sang before the Emperor. Throughout the palace, people listened to her sweet-sounding voice. Immediately, the

rain stopped and the water ran off the fields and they were no longer flooded. The Emperor felt much better and everyone was pleased with Princess Haya.

The only person who wasn't happy was Haya's mean stepmother. She told a servant to take Haya into the mountains and leave her there. So the servant took Haya, but he felt sorry for her. He built a cottage, and lived there with his wife and Princess Haya.

Haya's father was desperate to find his missing daughter, and he looked everywhere for her. One day he was out hunting in the mountains and came across a cottage. Princess Haya was in the garden singing, and when her father heard her beautiful voice he knew at once that it was his long-lost daughter.

"Dearest Haya!" he cried. When Haya saw her father she ran into his arms. She told him everything that her stepmother had done to her.

When her stepmother heard that Haya had been found, she ran away and was never heard of again. Princess Haya lived happily with her father. A few years later she married a handsome prince, and she became a kind and clever ruler.

The Twelve Brothers

Once there was a king and queen who had twelve sons. One day the king said to the queen, "If our thirteenth child is a girl, we must imprison our sons and give all our land and

possessions to our daughter."
This made the queen very
sad, so she came up with a plan
for her sons. "You must run
away into the woods and find
somewhere to hide where
no one can find you." So
the brothers ran away
and found a magic
house in the woods
where they lived for
the next ten years.

The Twelve Brothers

Meanwhile the King and queen had a baby girl. She grew up to be good and kind and always wore a gold star on her head. One day, when she was sixteen years old, the princess noticed twelve white shirts

drying on the washing line. She asked her mother who the shirts belonged to. The queen replied, "My dear, those shirts belong to your twelve brothers." The queen told the princess how

her brothers had been forced to
run away when she was a baby,
and the queen began to cry.

"Please don't cry mother,"
said the princess. "I will go and
find my brothers." She took the
twelve shirts and bravely set off
into the woods.

The princess walked all day,
and by night came to the house
in the woods where her brothers
lived. They asked her who she

was and why she was there. When the princess told them her story, the princes said that they were her long-lost brothers. So they all lived happily in the house in the woods, until one day something happened.

There was a garden around the house where twelve tall, white flowers grew. The princess wanted to give each brother a flower, so she picked them from

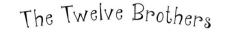

the garden. But as soon as she did this, the brothers were changed into ravens. They flew away over the woods, leaving their sister alone.

Suddenly, the princess saw an old

woman standing nearby so she asked, "How can I break the spell and free my brothers?" The old woman said, "You must not speak or make any sound for seven years." So the poor princess began her lonely life of silence.

One day, a few years later, a king came riding past the house and noticed the beautiful princess

with a gold star on her head as
she walked in the garden. He
asked her to be his wife. But as
the princess couldn't talk, she
simply nodded, and went with
the king to his palace where
they were married.

The king's mother didn't like
the princess and said nasty things
about her to the king. At first
the king didn't believe his mother.
But because the princess couldn't

speak and tell her husband the truth, he began to believe what his mother said. He decided to send the princess to prison.

Just as guards arrived to take the princess, the seven years came to an end – the spell was broken! Suddenly, twelve ravens flew down from the sky. The ravens turned back into the princess's brothers as they landed, and they quickly set

their sister free.
At last the
princess could
speak and
she told the king her
story. The king was so happy
when he heard that all the things
his mother had said weren't true.
His mother was sent away, and
everyone lived happily ever after.

This book
belongs to

....

First published in 2018 by Miles Kelly Publishing Ltd
Harding's Barn, Bardfield End Green, Thaxted, Essex, CM6 3PX, UK

2 4 6 8 10 9 7 5 3 1

Publishing Director Belinda Gallagher
Creative Director Jo Cowan
Editorial Director Rosie Neave
Senior Editor Becky Miles
Design Managers Joe Jones, Simon Lee
Image Manager Liberty Newton
Production Elizabeth Collins, Caroline Kelly
Reprographics Stephan Davis, Jennifer Cozens
Assets Lorraine King

ISBN 978-1-78617-477-2

Printed in China

British Library Cataloguing-in-Publication Data
A catalogue record for this book is available from the British Library

Acknowledgements

The publishers would like to thank the following artists who have contributed to this book:
Advocate Art: Natalia Moore
The Bright Agency: Maddie Frost (decorative frames), Clair Rossiter

Made with paper from a sustainable forest

www.mileskelly.net

Cinderella

♥

The Clever Tailor

MILES KELLY

Cinderella

There was once a rich man whose wife had died and left him with a young daughter. His daughter grew up to be good and kind.

Eventually, the rich man

married again. His new wife had two daughters who were mean to the rich man's daughter. They took away her pretty dresses and made her wear old, worn clothes and work in the kitchen.

They forced her to get up early to fetch wood to make the fire, and to wash all their clothes. At night, the sisters made her sleep by the fire in the coal dust, and because she was always so dusty with cinders they called her Cinderella.

One day a messenger came with an invitation from the King. There was going to be a grand ball over three days. The ball was for the prince, and all the ladies in the land were invited. The prince would choose a lady to marry at the end of the three days. The stepsisters were so excited! The ball was to start that evening, so they ordered Cinderella to help them get ready.

"Comb our hair, clean our shoes and button our dresses!" they shouted at poor Cinderella.

Cinderella

At last, Cinderella's
stepmother and sisters left for
the ball, leaving her alone with
lots of housework to do. Poor
Cinderella went outside and sat
down by a tree and cried. It was
so unfair that her stepsisters
could go to the ball when she
had chores to do.

Suddenly there was a flash
and a white dove flew down
from a tree. It was carrying

the most beautiful gold dress, and twinkling, sparkly shoes. Cinderella put them on and was whisked off to the ball.

The prince spotted Cinderella at once and asked her to dance. They danced together all evening. But Cinderella knew she had to

9

be home before her stepmother and sisters. So she slipped away when the prince wasn't looking and ran all the way home. The poor prince wondered where Cinderella had gone.

On the second day of the ball, after her stepmother and sisters had left, Cinderella sat by the tree again and the same thing happened. The dove brought her the most beautiful

dress and shoes and whisked
her off to the ball. The prince
was waiting for Cinderella, and
again he danced with her all
night. Once more, as it grew
late, Cinderella slipped away
and hurried home.

When her stepmother and
sisters returned, they talked
about the beautiful princess who
had danced with the prince all
night. They didn't know that the

princess was really Cinderella.

On the third day when her stepmother and sisters had gone to the ball, Cinderella again went outside to sit by the tree. This time the dove brought her an even more beautiful dress and shoes, and again the prince danced with her all evening.

But when Cinderella slipped away at the end of the night, one of her sparkly shoes came off her foot. The prince picked up the shoe and said, "I will marry the lady whose foot fits perfectly into this shoe."

The next morning the prince asked all the ladies of the land to come to the palace and try on the shoe. Cinderella's stepsisters pushed their way into the room where the shoe was. One at a time, they

Cinderella

squeezed their big, clumsy feet
into the little shoe but it was
clear that it didn't fit. Cinderella
came to the palace in her dirty
clothes. Her stepsisters laughed

at the thought of the shoe fitting her, but Cinderella's little foot slipped into the shoe perfectly. The prince looked at Cinderella's face and knew that this was the beautiful lady he had danced with at the ball.

"This is my bride," he cried. They were married the following day and lived happily ever after.

The Clever Tailor

Once upon a time there was a very proud, but clever princess. If a man asked to marry her she would give him a riddle. And when he couldn't guess the riddle he would be

The Clever Tailor

sent away. The princess said,
"I will only marry the man who
can guess my riddle."

One day three tailors went
to the palace and begged the

17

The Clever Tailor

princess to give them a riddle.
The princess said, "I have two
different colours of hair on my
head. What colours are they?"
The first tailor guessed black
and white, while the second
tailor guessed red and brown.
These answers were both
wrong. The third tailor who was
the youngest said, "The
princess has gold and silver
hair." The princess turned pale

as the tailor had got her
question right.

She said, "Don't think you
have won yet! You have still have
one more thing to do." And the
princess told the youngest tailor
that he had to sleep in a stable
with a bear for the night. She
knew that the bear had killed
everyone who had entered the
stable. "If you are still alive in
the morning, I will marry you,"

said the princess.

So the youngest tailor was taken to the stable. The bear had very sharp claws and was very fierce. It growled at the tailor. But the tailor said, "Be gentle," to the bear, and he started eating some nuts.

The bear wanted to eat nuts too, so he asked the tailor for some. But the tailor gave the bear pebbles instead of nuts.

The Clever Tailor

The bear found it hard to eat pebbles, and the tailor made fun of him. "What? You cannot crack a nut with those strong jaws of yours?"

Next, the tailor played a fiddle. The bear liked the music and started dancing. He asked the tailor how hard it was to play

The Clever Tailor

the fiddle. The tailor said it was easy, so the bear asked the tailor to teach him to play.

The tailor replied, "Your claws are very long. I must cut them first."

So the bear let the tailor tie his paws together so that he

could cut his claws. But instead
the tailor tied the bear's paws
so that he couldn't move! Then
the tailor went to sleep.

The next morning the
princess went to the stable
thinking that the bear would
have killed the tailor. But the
young tailor stood in front of the
stable door, smiling, and very
much alive! After this, the
princess knew she had met a

The Clever Tailor

man who was as clever as she
was. She married the tailor and
they both lived happily ever after.

This book belongs to

. . . .

First published in 2018 by Miles Kelly Publishing Ltd
Harding's Barn, Bardfield End Green, Thaxted, Essex, CM6 3PX, UK

2 4 6 8 10 9 7 5 3 1

Publishing Director Belinda Gallagher
Creative Director Jo Cowan
Editorial Director Rosie Neave
Senior Editor Becky Miles
Design Managers Joe Jones, Simon Lee
Image Manager Liberty Newton
Production Elizabeth Collins, Caroline Kelly
Reprographics Stephan Davis, Jennifer Cozens
Assets Lorraine King

ISBN 978-1-78617-479-6

Printed in China

British Library Cataloguing-in-Publication Data
A catalogue record for this book is available from the British Library

Acknowledgements

The publishers would like to thank the following artists who have contributed to this book:
The Bright Agency: Maddie Frost (decorative frames), Sarah Jennings, Clair Rossiter

Made with paper from a sustainable forest

www.mileskelly.net

Princess Rosette

♥

The Secret Princess

MILES
KELLY

Princess Rosette

Once upon a time there lived
a king and a queen who
had two handsome sons and
a beautiful baby daughter.

When it was time to christen
their daughter Rosette, they

invited the fairies. The queen asked them what would happen in her daughter's life. But the fairies didn't have good news.

"Because of her, Rosette's brothers will have bad luck."

The King and queen were worried about their sons. So they kept Rosette in a tower to stop her bringing any bad luck.

Many years later when the King and queen died, the eldest

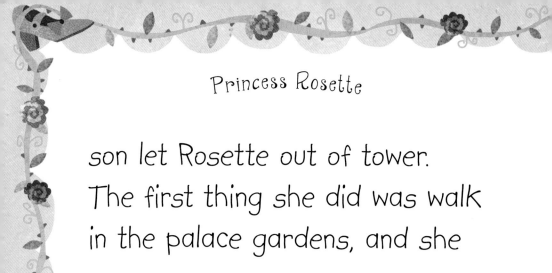

son let Rosette out of tower.
The first thing she did was walk
in the palace gardens, and she

was amazed by the colourful flowers growing there. She came across a beautiful peacock and said, "I will marry the King of the peacocks."

Her brothers laughed at her for saying she would marry a peacock! But they loved their sister, so they went in search of the king of the peacocks. After many weeks they found him! The princes showed the king a picture of their sister.

"She is the most beautiful princess in the world," the King said. So Rosette's brothers asked if he would marry her, and he said he would if she was as beautiful as her picture. But if she wasn't as beautiful, he would be very cross! Then the princes were put in prison until Rosette arrived.

The princess set off in a

boat to the Kingdom of the peacocks. She took her little dog named Frisk with her, and a maid. But not long into the journey the maid had a mean plan. When the princess was asleep she threw her bed, with the princess and Frisk still on it, into the sea. When the princess awoke she was terrified to find herself floating out to sea. She held on tight to the bed, with

Frisk sitting behind her.
Meanwhile the maid dressed
in the princess's clothes. She
met the king of the peacocks

and pretended that she was Princess Rosette. But the maid was not as beautiful as the princess, and when the King saw this, he was angry, as he thought the princes had tried to play a trick on him.

The princes were brought before the King to explain themselves. He wanted to know why they had lied, but the princes just said, "Please give us some time to prove to you that we are telling the truth."

Meanwhile, an old man had rescued Princess Rosette and Frisk from the sea. As the princess was feeling hungry, she tied a basket to Frisk and told him to bring back some food from the best kitchen he could find. Of course the best kitchen belonged to the king of peacocks.

So the little dog ran all the way to the king's kitchen and stole his food. This happened again and again, until the cook followed the little dog to the old man's cottage. Then he ran back to the king and told

him where all his dinners had gone. The King said he would like to go and see for himself who was stealing his food, so he went to the old man's cottage. He arrived just in time to see the princess and the old man finishing his dinner.

The princess told the King everything that had happened. The King realized that she was was the real Princess Rosette, and that the princes were telling the truth. Rosette was indeed as beautiful as her picture and the king fell in love with her. The princes were let out of prison, and Rosette and the king of peacocks were married.

The Secret Princess

Once upon a time there was a prince and princess who were happily married. But the prince decided to explore some faraway lands. So he said goodbye to his wife and set off on his travels. He visited many lands and had a great many adventures, but eventually was taken prisoner by a mean king.

The prince sent a message to his wife saying, "Come and rescue me from this prison." The princess thought if she went to rescue the prince then she too would be taken prisoner. But then she had an idea. She cut off her beautiful, long hair and dressed in boy's clothes. Then she took her lute and set off to rescue her husband.

The brave princess travelled through many lands dressed as a boy and playing her lute, before she reached the palace where the prince was in prison. She went into the palace and played her lute and sang as beautifully as she could. The mean king listened, and thought it was the loveliest sound he had ever heard. He told her, "Stay here and play for a few days. When you leave I will give you whatever you ask for."

The Secret Princess

So the princess stayed for three days, then she asked the King for one of his prisoners. "It will be nice to have a friend to travel with," she said. So the King allowed the princess to choose a prisoner, and she chose her husband, although she pretended not to know him.

The couple set off on the long journey home. But the princess was still dressed as a boy and the prince didn't realize he was travelling with his wife. Although he asked many questions, he never found out who she was. All the time the secret princess was leading him back home.

When they were almost at the palace, the princess slipped away. She took a short cut and arrived before the prince. She changed into a beautiful dress and waited outside the palace. As the prince arrived, a crowd was cheering, "Our prince is home!" But the prince was angry with his wife because he thought she hadn't helped him.

So as the prince was talking to his people, the princess slipped away again and changed back into boy's clothing. Then she came and stood before her husband and started playing the

lute and singing sweetly.

The prince realized that his wife was really disguised as the lute player all along, and that she had rescued him. He was sorry that he had doubted her. The prince put on a great feast for his wife, and everyone celebrated for a week.

This book
belongs to

....

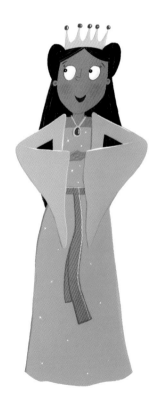

First published in 2018 by Miles Kelly Publishing Ltd
Harding's Barn, Bardfield End Green, Thaxted, Essex, CM6 3PX, UK

Copyright © Miles Kelly Publishing Ltd 2018

2 4 6 8 10 9 7 5 3 1

Publishing Director Belinda Gallagher
Creative Director Jo Cowan
Editorial Director Rosie Neave
Senior Editor Becky Miles
Design Managers Joe Jones, Simon Lee
Image Manager Liberty Newton
Production Elizabeth Collins, Caroline Kelly
Reprographics Stephan Davis, Jennifer Cozens
Assets Lorraine King

ISBN 978-1-78617-488-8

Printed in China

British Library Cataloguing-in-Publication Data
A catalogue record for this book is available from the British Library

Acknowledgements

The publishers would like to thank the following artists who have contributed to this book:
The Bright Agency: Charlotte Cooke, Maddie Frost (decorative frames), Maxine Lee

Made with paper from a sustainable forest

www.mileskelly.net

The
Wise
Girl

♥

The
Princess
and the
Pea

MILES KELLY

The Wise Girl

There was once a girl who was wiser than the King. Her father was so proud of her that he told everyone how clever she was. One day he said, "My daughter is so clever that she could answer any question that the king asked."

The King heard about this, and the next day he gave the man thirty eggs for his daughter to hatch. The King said, "Only a clever person could make these eggs hatch." So the man gave the eggs to his daughter, but the girl realized that the eggs had been boiled and would not hatch. But her

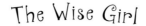

father was afraid to take them back to the King.

The girl gave her father a bag of boiled beans. She told him to pretend to plant the beans by the road when the King passed by. The King didn't recognize the man. He stopped and said, "My poor man, how can you think boiled beans will grow?"

The man replied as his daughter had instructed him:

"Whatever the king asks can be done. If boiled eggs can hatch into chickens, then why can't boiled beans grow?" The king remembered giving the eggs to the man the day before. The king was surprised at the clever girl's answer. He sent for the girl to come to the palace.

She stood in front of the king in her plain dress and old shoes. The king was happy with her

The Wise Girl

answers and knew he wanted
her to be his queen. But the girl
said, "I am poor and we may

not be happy. You may want to send me back to my father. Promise me that if this happens I can take home what is most dear to me." The king agreed, and they were married.

After she became queen the girl wore beautiful dresses and jewels. But the king grew jealous and thought she cared more about her dresses than him. He told her to go back to her father.

But the girl wanted to take with her the thing she held most dear. She gave the king a drink with some sleeping powder in it. He fell asleep immediately, and the girl arranged for servants to take him to her old home.

When the king awoke, he was surprised to be in her father's

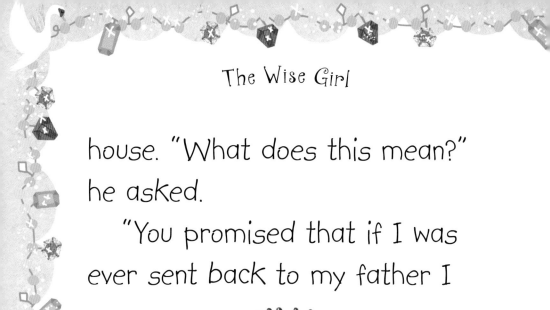

house. "What does this mean?" he asked.

"You promised that if I was ever sent back to my father I

could take with me the thing that was most dear to me. Well, I've taken you because you are the most dear to me!"

Of course after that, the king wasn't jealous or angry any more. They went back to the palace and lived together in great happiness.

The Princess and the Pea

There was once a prince who wanted to get married. But his future wife had to behave like a real princess.

So the prince travelled all over the world looking for his

princess. He looked everywhere, and visited many different lands. And although he was invited to lots of palaces and met many princesses, he couldn't tell if they were real princesses. There always seemed to be something not quite right about all the young ladies he met.

One evening when the prince was back at home, there was a terrible storm. Thunder crashed

and lightning flashed as the rain
poured down. Suddenly there
was a knock at the palace
gates. The old King went to see
who was calling at that time of
the night.

The King was very surprised
to see a princess standing
outside. She was wet through,
water dripped from her hair
and clothes, and her shoes were
covered in mud. She didn't look

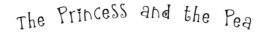

like a princess at all. Yet she
told the king that
she was!

The king
couldn't leave the
poor girl standing
in the rain.
So she was
invited in
and offered
some hot
milk and a

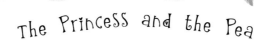

blanket to keep her warm.

"You may stay the night, my dear," he said.

The queen looked at the girl and didn't think she was a real princess, either. "We shall soon find out," said the queen, and she went away to prepare a room for the girl to sleep in.

The queen went to a guest bedroom and ordered her maids to remove the mattress and all

the bed covers from the bed.
Then the queen placed a tiny
pea on the bedstead and
instructed the maids to pile
twenty mattresses and twenty
bed covers on top of the little
pea. The bed was so high that
it reached the ceiling!

The queen then showed the
princess to her room. She gave
her some clean night clothes
to put on and wished her

goodnight. The princess needed
a ladder to climb to the
top of the bed!

In the morning the
queen asked the

princess how she had slept.
"Very badly!" said the princess.
And when the queen asked
her why, she said, "I was
kept awake most of the

night *by* something very hard and lumpy in the bed."

When she heard this, it was clear to the queen that the girl was indeed a real princess. As only a real princess was so delicate that she could feel a tiny little pea through twenty mattresses and twenty bed covers.

So the prince married the real princess. And the pea was

kept in a special glass case in the palace, where it can still be seen today.

THE PEA

This book
belongs to

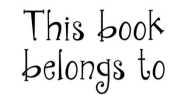

. . . .

First published in 2018 by Miles Kelly Publishing Ltd
Harding's Barn, Bardfield End Green, Thaxted, Essex, CM6 3PX, UK

Copyright © Miles Kelly Publishing Ltd 2018

2 4 6 8 10 9 7 5 3 1

Publishing Director Belinda Gallagher
Creative Director Jo Cowan
Editorial Director Rosie Neave
Senior Editor Becky Miles
Design Managers Joe Jones, Simon Lee
Image Manager Liberty Newton
Production Elizabeth Collins, Caroline Kelly
Reprographics Stephan Davis, Jennifer Cozens
Assets Lorraine King

ISBN 978-1-78617-486-4

Printed in China

British Library Cataloguing-in-Publication Data
A catalogue record for this book is available from the British Library

Acknowledgements

The publishers would like to thank the following artists who have contributed to this book:
The Bright Agency: Maddie Frost (decorative frames), Clair Rossiter, Louise Wright

Made with paper from a sustainable forest

www.mileskelly.net

The Dreadful Giant

♥

The Princess, the Wooden Dress, and the Comb

MILES KELLY

The Dreadful Giant

One day, a princess was playing catch with her ball in the garden. She threw the ball much higher than ever before, and it never came down.

"Aargh!" a loud voice roared

The Dreadful Giant

from high up in the sky.
Suddenly, a palace guard
appeared and whisked the
princess away to a castle on a
mountain. He took
her to a tower
that was filled
with white cats.

The Dreadful Giant

"Your ball hit a giant in the eye, and that was the giant you heard shouting," said the guard. He told the princess that giants hate white cats, so to keep her safe, she would now live at the Castle of the White Cats.

The princess was so happy playing with the cats that she soon forgot about the giant. But the giant hadn't forgotten about her. "Cats love mice better than

princesses," the giant said. So
he filled a large sack with
hundreds of fat mice and went
to the castle.

The princess could see a long
way from her tower, and she
spotted the giant heading
towards the castle with a large
sack. The clever princess
guessed what the giant was
carrying. "I will give you
hundreds more mice and much

fatter mice than the giant," she told the cats.

When the giant let the mice out of the sack they ran all over the castle, but the cats didn't chase after them. They could hear the mice and smell the mice, but not one cat moved! So the giant returned home in a very bad mood.

"Cats love sparrows more than princesses," said the giant.

The Dreadful Giant

So this time he filled a big cage with lots of fat sparrows. But once again the princess saw the giant coming to the castle from her tower, and she guessed what he was planning.

9

The Dreadful Giant

"I will give you hundreds more sparrows, and much fatter ones than the giant," the princess said to the cats. So again when the giant released the sparrows over the castle, not one cat moved. And the giant went home again huffing and puffing with anger.

Next the giant got some magic powder from a wise frog. When he poured water onto the powder it turned blue. So the giant set off to the castle with a large jug of blue water. But again the clever princess was one step ahead of him.

When the giant reached the castle, he shut his eyes (because giants don't like

looking at white cats)
and poured the blue
water over the cats.
He also slopped blue
water all over himself. So the
white cats, and the giant, turned
bright blue. But at least the
giant could open his eyes. He
stomped up to the highest room
in the castle and burst in. But
the clever princess was nowhere
to be seen.

The Dreadful Giant

A fairy had
flown over the palace
as the giant approached with
the blue water. The princess
asked for her help, so the fairy
changed the princess into a tiny
flea, which meant the giant
couldn't see her.

The blue giant stormed out

of the castle grunting and muttering. He was so angry that he didn't look where he was going, and he walked right off the edge of the mountain – and that was the end of the dreadful giant.

Meanwhile, the fairy changed the flea back into the princess, and all the cats were given a bubble bath to get the blue colour out of their fur. In no

The Dreadful Giant

time they were pure white again,
and they lived happily ever after
in the castle with the princess.

The Princess, the Wooden Dress, and the Comb

Long ago there was a little princess and her father loved her very much. She was very pretty and loved looking at her face in the glassy waters of pools in the woods. But

sometimes the little princess
was very naughty
and her temper
was not as lovely
as her face.

She would play
in the sand and
roll around in
the woods
among the
leaves and
bushes until

17

her beautiful curls were all
tangled up.

Her maid combed her hair
with a stone comb – for they
only had combs made of stone
in those days – and she would
groan and moan and stamp her
foot. When the princess was
very angry she would even call
her maid an elephant! When she
did this, her poor maid would
put her hands up to her face to

feel if she had an elephant's trunk!

One day the princess would rule the land, and the king was worried that his naughty daughter wouldn't grow up to be good and kind.

When the king was out walking in the woods one day, a gentle wind rustled the leaves of an oak tree, and the tree said, "Make a dress out of my branches. When your daughter is naughty, make her wear the dress until she is good."

Next, a huge stag came into the woods. The stag said to the king, "Make

20

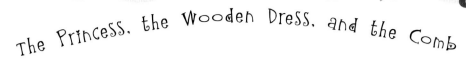

a comb out of one
of my antlers and
use it to comb the
princess's hair.
It will be
softer than
the stone
comb."
So the
king had a
wooden
dress made

from the oak tree, and whenever the princess was naughty she had to wear it. The princess didn't like wearing the dress, as it was hard and uncomfortable, and the other children laughed at her. But the dress didn't stop the princess from being naughty.

The king also had a comb made from one of the stag's antlers for the princess to use instead of the stone comb. And then a very strange thing happened. Every time the maid combed the princess's hair with the antler comb, the princess was sweet and good. She often thanked her maid and said she liked to have her curls brushed and smoothed. She even asked to comb her own hair.

In fact, such a change came over the princess that soon she didn't wear the wooden dress much after using the comb, and before long she didn't need to wear it at all.

This book belongs to

. . . .

First published in 2018 by Miles Kelly Publishing Ltd
Harding's Barn, Bardfield End Green, Thaxted, Essex, CM6 3PX, UK

2 4 6 8 10 9 7 5 3 1

Publishing Director Belinda Gallagher
Creative Director Jo Cowan
Editorial Director Rosie Neave
Senior Editor Becky Miles
Design Managers Joe Jones, Simon Lee
Image Manager Liberty Newton
Production Elizabeth Collins, Caroline Kelly
Reprographics Stephan Davis, Jennifer Cozens
Assets Lorraine King

ISBN 978-1-78617-490-1

Printed in China

British Library Cataloguing-in-Publication Data
A catalogue record for this book is available from the British Library

Acknowledgements

The publishers would like to thank the following artists who have contributed to this book:
The Bright Agency: Smiljana Coh, Maddie Frost (decorative frames), Sarah Jennings

All other artwork from the Miles Kelly Artwork Bank

Made with paper from a sustainable forest

www.mileskelly.net

The Twelve Dancing Princessess

♥

The Flower Princess

Miles Kelly

The Twelve Dancing Princesses

There once was a King who had twelve beautiful daughters. They slept in twelve beds all in one big room and when they went to bed each night their bedroom door was

locked. But every morning their shoes were worn out, as if they had been dancing all night long. The king was at his wits end and said, "Whoever can find out where the princesses go at night can choose a princess to marry."

Many princes had a go at guessing the clever princesses' secret. One night, a prince was even given a room next door to the princesses' bedroom. He left his door open so that he could see if they left their room. He should have kept watch all night, but soon fell fast asleep. In the morning he discovered that the princesses had been dancing all night again, and that their shoes were quite worn out.

One day a soldier was passing through the town when he met an old woman. He told her that he wanted to find out the princesses' secret.

"Then you must not drink the milk that the eldest princess will give you," said the old woman. "When she leaves, you must just pretend to be asleep."

Then the old woman gave the

soldier a cloak and told him that
when he put it on he
would be invisible.

The soldier
arrived at the
palace and was
shown to the
room next to
the princesses'
bedroom. Just
as he was
settling down,

the eldest princess brought him
a glass of milk. When she
wasn't looking the soldier tipped
the milk away and then
pretended to fall asleep. The
princess laughed and went back
to her sisters. The soldier heard
the princesses giggling in their
bedroom as they excitedly got
dressed to go dancing.

When the princesses were
ready they checked the soldier

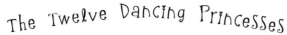

was asleep. He was snoring, so
they went back into their room
and the eldest princess clapped
her hands. A trapdoor opened,
and the princesses
hurried down
some steps.

The soldier saw all of this as he had only pretended to be asleep. He jumped up, put on the magic cloak and quickly followed the princesses down the steps. The youngest princess thought she heard someone behind her. But the cloak made the soldier invisible so she couldn't see him.

The steps led to a lake upon which beautiful swans were

swimming, and where twelve boats with twelve princes were waiting for the princesses. The soldier hopped into the boat with the eldest princess.

They reached the other side of the lake where a glittering castle stood. The invisible soldier followed the princesses and the princes inside, where they danced all night until their shoes were worn out. Then the soldier followed as the princes rowed the princesses back across the lake and said goodbye.

The soldier ran up the steps ahead of the princesses and lay

down in his room and snored.
When the princesses returned
they heard him snoring and
said, "We are safe."

The next morning the king
asked the soldier where his
daughters went to dance at
night. The soldier said, "They
dance with twelve princes in a
castle underground." And he told
the king what he had seen.

The princesses knew their

secret was out and told their
father it was true. The King
asked the soldier which princess
he would like to marry.

"I would like to marry the
eldest princess, if she will marry
me." The princess was happy to
marry a man as clever as her,
and they lived happily ever after.

The Flower Princess

There was once a princess so fair and lovely that the sun shone more brightly on her than on anyone else, the river stopped running when she walked by so that it might gaze

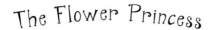

on her beauty, and birds sang underneath her window at night.

Princes came to beg for her hand in marriage, but she swore she would only marry a prince who was kind, good and true. Many princes tried to convince her of their fine qualities, but none succeeded – until one day a prince from a small kingdom came to woo her. He fell in love with her, she could not resist

him, and they were married.
She wore a silver dress
embroidered with crystal drops
and looked lovely. The court
scattered her path with rose
petals and threw sugar sweets
as the couple walked past.

But alas, trouble can come to all of us. The prince's Kingdom had an evil fairy. She was very beautiful but her beauty was spoilt by the cruelty and mean thoughts that she held inside.

When she saw the princess with her sweet and good face, her heart filled with jealousy and rage. She wove a spell to transform the princess into a flower in a nearby meadow.

But the spell was
not powerful
enough to
conquer the
princess completely.
Each night she appeared again
in her true form, but every
morning she had to transform
into her flowery shape and
spend the day standing among
the grasses and the other
flowers in the meadow.

21

One night she overheard the fairy talking and learnt how to break the spell. She told her husband, "If you come to the meadow in the morning and pick me the spell will be broken forever."

"How will I know which one is you?" he said. The princess did not know, for her shape changed every day.

That morning she changed

into a flower and the prince
hastened to the field to try and
find his love. He walked among
the grasses and the many
flowers. How could he find
his love?

Then a thought came to him
and he looked closely at each
bloom. Finally he stopped before
a blue cornflower, touched it
gently with his fingers, plucked
it and carried it back to his

palace. As he passed through the gates, the flower fell to the ground and his princess stood before him.

"How did you find me?" she asked.

"Dew had fallen on all of the other flowers," he replied, "you alone had no dew upon you, for you had spent the night at the palace."

This book
belongs to

. . . .

First published in 2018 by Miles Kelly Publishing Ltd
Harding's Barn, Bardfield End Green, Thaxted, Essex, CM6 3PX, UK

Copyright © Miles Kelly Publishing Ltd 2018

2 4 6 8 10 9 7 5 3 1

Publishing Director Belinda Gallagher
Creative Director Jo Cowan
Editorial Director Rosie Neave
Senior Editor Becky Miles
Design Managers Joe Jones, Simon Lee
Image Manager Liberty Newton
Production Elizabeth Collins, Caroline Kelly
Reprographics Stephan Davis, Jennifer Cozens
Assets Lorraine King

ISBN 978-1-78617-481-9

Printed in China

British Library Cataloguing-in-Publication Data
A catalogue record for this book is available from the British Library

Acknowledgements

The publishers would like to thank the following artists who have contributed to this book:
The Bright Agency: Rosie Butcher, Maddie Frost (decorative frames), Maxine Lee

Made with paper from a sustainable forest

www.mileskelly.net

Sleeping Beauty

♥

The Crow

Miles Kelly

Sleeping Beauty

Once upon a time in a faraway land, a king and queen had a beautiful baby girl. They arranged a feast and invited many guests to celebrate the baby's arrival. The queen said,

"I will invite the fairies, too, so they will be kind to our little daughter." So they invited twelve fairies but they didn't ask the thirteenth fairy because she was so mean.

After the feast, the fairies stood around the baby princess's cradle. Each fairy waved her wand and gave a special gift to the princess, such as goodness, kindness and happiness.

Sleeping Beauty

Suddenly, just before the last
fairy was about to give her gift,
the door burst open.
It was the
thirteenth

fairy. She was angry because she hadn't been invited, and she went up to the baby and said, "When the princess is fifteen she will prick her finger on a spindle and die!"

The king and queen were very upset when they heard this, and the mean fairy flew off. But everyone had forgotten that the last fairy had still to give her gift. She stepped

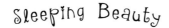

forward and said, "I cannot take away the bad wish, but I can change it."

So the last fairy said that when the princess pricked her finger she would not die, but would instead fall asleep for one hundred years. All the people in the palace would fall asleep, too. So when the princess woke up, her family and friends would all be there too.

The princess grew up to be good, kind and happy, all of the things that the fairies had said she would be. But on the day of her fifteenth birthday, the princess decided to explore an old part of the palace. She found a door that she hadn't seen before, with a gold key in the lock. The princess turned the key and slowly the door creaked open.

Inside the room sat an old woman, who was spinning wool. The old lady was really the mean fairy in disguise. The princess asked, "What are you doing?" And as she did so, she touched the spindle and pricked her finger.

10

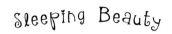

At once, the princess fell into a deep sleep. And just as the fairy had wished, the king, queen and everyone else in the palace fell asleep, too.

Over many years, a thorny hedge grew all around the palace. It grew so thick and high that soon no part of the palace could be seen.

People forgot that it was there.

Then one day, exactly one hundred years later, a prince was riding by. He caught a glimpse of the palace and used an axe to chop his way through the thorny hedge. The palace was dusty and covered in cobwebs and there were people sleeping everywhere. Even the pigeons on the roof had their heads tucked under their wings.

The prince walked further until he came to the door with the golden key. He turned the key and found the princess sleeping inside. She looked so beautiful that the prince bent down and kissed her.

At that moment, the spell was broken and the princess opened her eyes. The prince and princess fell in love at first sight. Then everyone in the palace woke up. The pigeons lifted their heads from under their wings, the horses shook themselves, and the dogs jumped up and barked.

The prince and princess went in search of the king and queen to ask if they could get married. Of course the king and queen agreed, and a week later the wedding took place. Everyone came to the wedding, including the fairies. But of course the bad fairy wasn't invited!

15

The Crow

Once upon a time there were three princesses. They were all beautiful but the youngest was the kindest. There was an old castle near the princesses' palace, which had a lovely flower

The Crow

garden. The youngest princess loved to go walking there.

One day, the princess was in the garden and a crow hopped in front of her. The poor crow was bleeding and its feathers were torn. This made the

princess sad. But the crow said to her, "I am really a prince who has been changed into a crow by a witch."

The crow asked the princess to leave her home and live with him in the old castle to break the spell. At once the kind princess agreed. She said goodbye to her family and went to live in the old castle. She was given a room with a golden bed, and the crow said to her, "You must not make a sound at night, no matter what you see."

When night came the princess was afraid, and she couldn't sleep. Then at midnight, her door was flung open and a huge green dragon came in. It breathed hot fire near the princess's bed. But she lay still and didn't make a sound.

The dragon disappeared and

next a big brown bear stomped
into the room. The bear roared,
showing its sharp teeth. Still the
princess was quiet. Next a huge
monster came in and leapt

20

The Crow

towards the princess, but she
remained still and quiet.
Then the monster, too,
disappeared. For
many nights,
strange creatures
came into the
princess's room
but the princess
was brave and
didn't make a
sound. The crow

21

thanked the princess for being so brave and told her he was getting better.

One day the crow said, "Soon I shall be free from this wicked spell. But now I need you to work as a maid for a while." So the princess did as she was asked. The people she worked for were unkind and made the princess work hard. But still she carried on.

Then one evening while the princess was at her spinning wheel and her hands were very sore from spinning all day, a young man knelt beside her and kissed her hands.

"I am the prince who was once the crow you helped," he said. "Your kindness has finally freed me from the wicked spell."

The prince took the princess back to the crumbling castle – but it was not an old castle anymore. It had been repaired and painted, and was now a beautiful, shining palace. The prince and princess were married and lived there happily for the rest of their days.

This book
belongs to

. . . .

First published in 2018 by Miles Kelly Publishing Ltd
Harding's Barn, Bardfield End Green, Thaxted, Essex, CM6 3PX, UK

2 4 6 8 10 9 7 5 3 1

Publishing Director Belinda Gallagher
Creative Director Jo Cowan
Editorial Director Rosie Neave
Senior Editor Becky Miles
Design Managers Joe Jones, Simon Lee
Image Manager Liberty Newton
Production Elizabeth Collins, Caroline Kelly
Reprographics Stephan Davis, Jennifer Cozens
Assets Lorraine King

ISBN 978-1-78617-476-5

Printed in China

British Library Cataloguing-in-Publication Data
A catalogue record for this book is available from the British Library

Acknowledgements

The publishers would like to thank the following artists who have contributed to this book:
The Bright Agency: Louise Ellis, Maddie Frost (decorative frames) Maxine Lee

Made with paper from a sustainable forest

www.mileskelly.net

The Little Mermaid

The Pig Boy

MiLeS KeLLY

The Little Mermaid

In a castle deep under the sea lived a sea king and his six daughters, who were sea princesses, or mermaids. The youngest mermaid was the most beautiful, with eyes as blue as

the sea. Like her sisters she had no legs or feet and her body ended in a shimmering, green fishtail.

Outside the castle was a beautiful garden of bright, colourful sea flowers. Each of the mermaid princesses had a little plot of ground in the garden that was theirs to tend. The youngest mermaid loved nothing more than looking after

her flowers as she gazed at a stone statue of a boy that had fallen to the bottom of the sea long ago.

She also loved listening to her grandmother's stories of the world above the sea.

"When you are fifteen," said her grandmother, "you can go above the sea and sit on the rocks in the moonlight." The youngest princess longed to see the world above the sea. "I wish I was fifteen years old right now," she said. "I know I will love

7

the world above, and all the people who live in it."

At last the youngest princess turned fifteen. She waved goodbye to her sisters and rose as lightly as a bubble to the top of the sea. A large ship sat on the water. The little mermaid swam as close to the ship as she dared, and when the waves lifted her she could see the people onboard.

The Little Mermaid

She saw a young prince with dark eyes. It was his sixteenth birthday and there was dancing and fireworks. The fireworks frightened the little mermaid and she dived back under the sea. But then she came up again as she couldn't keep her eyes off the beautiful prince.

After a while the ship set sail. But suddenly a storm came from nowhere. The waves were so high, and the ship was tossed up and down. Suddenly, the prince was thrown into the sea. The little mermaid swam to help him and held his head

above the water. She swam
with the prince to land and laid
him on the beach. The prince
started to wake up, but the little
mermaid had to return to her
father's castle under the sea.
The prince didn't know that she
had saved him.

From then on, the little
mermaid would spend many
nights in the water near the
prince's palace to watch him.

She wished more than anything
that she could live in his world.

So one day she went to the
sea witch who lived in deep,
dark water. The little mermaid
had never been to that part of
the sea before. She was so
scared that she almost changed
her mind. But then she thought
of how much she wanted to be
with the prince above the sea.

"I know what you want," said

The Little Mermaid

the sea witch, and she gave the
little mermaid a special drink.
She told her to swim to land,

and then take the drink. "Your tail will disappear and you will grow legs," said the sea witch. "But once you are a person you can never be a mermaid again. And if the prince marries another, you will die!"

The little mermaid also had to give the sea witch her voice in return for the special drink, so she could never speak again. At last she swam up to the prince's

palace and took the drink. Her tail disappeared and she grew legs. When the prince found her on the beach, he took her back to his palace and made sure she was well cared for and dressed in fine clothes.

The little mermaid and the prince spent all their time together, and the prince said she would always be by his side. As time passed the little mermaid loved the prince more and more, and he loved her. But he didn't think of her as a wife.

Then one day the prince sailed away to meet a princess who his parents wanted him to marry. The little mermaid went too. When the prince saw the princess, he fell in love with her, and they were married.

When everyone was having fun at the wedding, the little

mermaid blew the prince a kiss
and slipped away into the sea.
But she did not die. Instead she
was lifted up by spirits, and
flew around the world
with them doing
good deeds.

The Pig Boy

There was once a prince who wanted to marry a certain princess. So he sent her two gifts. The first was a sweet-smelling rose. But when the princess received the rose, she cried, "Ugh!" The second gift was a nightingale, which sang sweetly. But when the princess heard the bird, she cried, "Go away!"

The prince didn't give up. He put on some scruffy clothes to disguise himself, and went to the palace to ask for work. He was given a job as a Pig Boy looking

after the King's pigs.

One evening after working all day, the Pig Boy put some bells around a cooking pot. When the pot boiled, it shook the bells and made a tune. The princess heard the tune. She wanted that pot! So her maid asked the Pig Boy what he wanted in return for it. He said, "A kiss from the princess."

The princess wanted the pot so much that she agreed. She

told her ladies to crowd round
so no one could see. Then she
gave the Pig Boy a kiss.

The next day the Pig Boy
made a rattle that played music.
The princess heard his rattle
and wanted that, too. Again she
told her maid to ask the Pig Boy
what he wanted for his rattle.
This time he said, "I want two
kisses from the princess." The
princess wanted the rattle so

much that she agreed. Her ladies stood round her again whilst she kissed the Pig Boy twice.

Meanwhile, the King was looking for his daughter. He was shocked to find her kissing the Pig Boy, and made her leave the palace.

22

The Pig Boy

"If only I had married the prince who sent me the gifts," wailed the princess as she set off alone.

But the Pig Boy ran ahead of her. He hid behind a tree and put on his fine royal clothes. Then he stepped out in front of the princess. "I am that prince," he said to her. "But I don't like you very much now. You were too selfish to see how beautiful a

rose smelled or how lovely a nightingale sang. Yet you were happy to kiss a pig boy to get what you wanted."

So the two went their separate ways, and the prince eventually found a princess who appreciated his gifts, and who was thoughtful and kind.

This book belongs to

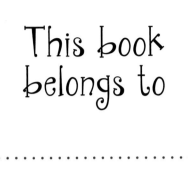

. . . .

First published in 2018 by Miles Kelly Publishing Ltd
Harding's Barn, Bardfield End Green, Thaxted, Essex, CM6 3PX, UK

Copyright © Miles Kelly Publishing Ltd 2018

2 4 6 8 10 9 7 5 3 1

Publishing Director Belinda Gallagher
Creative Director Jo Cowan
Editorial Director Rosie Neave
Senior Editor Becky Miles
Design Managers Joe Jones, Simon Lee
Image Manager Liberty Newton
Production Elizabeth Collins, Caroline Kelly
Reprographics Stephan Davis, Jennifer Cozens
Assets Lorraine King

ISBN 978-1-78617-483-3

Printed in China

British Library Cataloguing-in-Publication Data
A catalogue record for this book is available from the British Library

Acknowledgements

The publishers would like to thank the following artists who have contributed to this book:
Advocate Art: Natalia Moore
The Bright Agency: Maddie Frost (decorative frames), Clair Rossiter

Made with paper from a sustainable forest

www.mileskelly.net

The Iron Oven

♥

The Ruby Prince

Miles Kelly

The Iron Oven

A long time ago a witch put a wicked spell on a prince and shut him in a large iron oven in the woods.

One day a princess, who was lost in the woods, came across

the oven. She was shocked to hear a voice coming from inside it. The voice said, "I am a prince and can help you find your way home."

In return for helping the princess get home, the prince asked her to return with a knife to help free him from the oven. The prince also said that he would marry the princess if she helped him.

So the princess did everything the prince asked. Then she made a hole in the oven with the knife and worked hard until the hole was big enough for the prince to climb out of. He was very handsome and the princess fell in love with him at once. He asked her to go with him to his castle and get

married. But the princess
wanted to tell her father the
happy news.

The Iron Oven

"Very well," said the prince, "but be careful, as you must not speak more than three words, if you do, the spell I am under cannot be broken."

The princess said she wouldn't, and ran back to her father. But as soon as she got home, she was so excited that she spoke more than three words. Immediately a wind blew any memory of the princess from the prince's head, and sent him back to his castle. When the princess ran back into the woods she couldn't find the prince anywhere.

After nine days of looking for the prince, the princess found a little house in the woods, which was home to a family of toads. The princess explained what had happened, and the toads told her where she could find the

The Iron Oven

prince's palace. They gave her a magic nut and told her to open it whenever she needed help. Then they wished her good luck.

The brave princess travelled over a glass mountain, a field with plants as sharp as swords and a huge lake. At last she reached the prince's castle. But after walking for so long the princess's clothes were dirty and torn, and she didn't look like a

princess at all. How could she
go to the castle to see
her prince looking
like that? Suddenly,
the princess

remembered the magic nut that the kind toads had given to her. She used a stone to prise open the nut. Inside was the most beautiful dress she had ever seen – it was made of glittering gold and shone like the sun.

The princess put on the dress and knocked at the castle gates. As soon as the prince saw her he remembered who she was, and threw his arms around her. The spell was broken! They were married that day, and lived happily ever after.

The Ruby Prince

There once was a king who was given a beautiful red, ruby stone. The stone was wrapped in cotton wool and locked in a chest. After twelve years the king wanted to see his

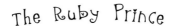

ruby, so the chest was brought
before him and unlocked. To
everyone's surprise a young man
jumped out.
"Who are
you?" asked
the King. "And
where is my
ruby?"

15

The Ruby Prince

The young man replied, "I am the Ruby Prince."

When the king's daughter and the Ruby Prince met, they fell in love. They were married and given half of the king's land.

The princess loved her handsome husband but was sad because she didn't know anything about him. Every day she asked her husband where he was from, but every day he

said, "I cannot tell you that."
Then one day, the Ruby
Prince and the princess were
walking by a lake. The
princess begged her
husband to tell her
where he was
from. Suddenly
there appeared a
giant snake
wearing a

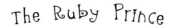

golden crown, and in a puff the
Ruby Prince was gone.

The princess went home with
a heavy heart. She offered a
reward to anyone who could tell
her where her Ruby Prince had
gone. Weeks went by with no
news. Then one day, a dancing-
girl told the princess what had
happened when she was
collecting wood and had fallen
asleep by a tree.

"I woke up and saw some young men coming out of a hole in the tree. They wore jewels and danced before a snake king. One man wore a red ruby and looked sad."

The next night the princess went with the dancing-girl

to the tree. Just as the girl had said, some men came out of the tree, and one man was wearing a ruby. The princess recognized her husband, the Ruby Prince, but she was sad to see he was so unhappy. Every night after that, the princess went to the tree to watch her husband, and every night she was sad that she couldn't speak to him.

But the clever princess came

up with a plan. She said, "The snake king loves dancing. What if I was able to dance beautifully for him? He may give me anything I ask for!" So the princess asked the dancing-girl to teach her how to dance. She was very graceful, and was soon better than the dancing-girl herself.

One night, the princess dressed in a beautiful gown and

sparkling jewels so that she
shone like a star. She hid
behind the tree and waited for
the men to come out. When

22

they appeared, the Ruby Prince looked sadder than ever. The princess stepped out from behind the tree and danced before the snake king.

The snake king cried out, "O dancer that no one knows, ask for anything and it will be yours." The princess asked for the Ruby Prince. The snake king knew he had been tricked. But he said, "Take him and go!"

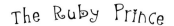

The Ruby Prince

So the princess and the Ruby Prince ran home, where they lived happily every after. And the princess never asked the Ruby Prince where he came from again.

This book
belongs to

. . . .

First published in 2018 by Miles Kelly Publishing Ltd
Harding's Barn, Bardfield End Green, Thaxted, Essex, CM6 3PX, UK

2 4 6 8 10 9 7 5 3 1

Publishing Director Belinda Gallagher
Creative Director Jo Cowan
Editorial Director Rosie Neave
Senior Editor Becky Miles
Design Managers Joe Jones, Simon Lee
Image Manager Liberty Newton
Production Elizabeth Collins, Caroline Kelly
Reprographics Stephan Davis, Jennifer Cozens
Assets Lorraine King

ISBN 978-1-78617-493-2

Printed in China

British Library Cataloguing-in-Publication Data
A catalogue record for this book is available from the British Library

Acknowledgements

The publishers would like to thank the following artists who have contributed to this book:
The Bright Agency: Mélanie Florian, Maddie Frost (decorative frames), Sarah Jennings

Made with paper from a sustainable forest

www.mileskelly.net

The Shepherd's Posy

The Blacksmith's Daughter

MILES KELLY

The Shepherd's Posy

There was once a King who had a beautiful daughter. A time came when she wanted to get married, so the King invited the princes of the land to come and meet her. But one prince wanted to see her before all the others did. He disguised himself as a shepherd and set off for the palace, taking some bread to eat on his journey.

On the way he met a poor man who asked him for something to eat. The kind prince gladly gave his bread to the man who thanked him and gave him three magic gifts in return. These were a spade, a net and a flute.

The Shepherd's Posy

When the prince arrived at the palace he was still dressed as a shepherd. He said his name was Yan and asked for work. He was given the king's sheep to look after, so he took them to a field, and planted the magic spade upright next to them. The sheep would always stay by the spade.

Then Yan went in search of a castle that he knew belonged to a giant. "Good afternoon," Yan said to the giant when he found the castle. But the giant wanted to eat Yan for his dinner. Quick as a flash, Yan threw his magic net over the giant, who toppled to the ground.

Yan escaped through the giant's garden, which was filled with the most beautiful flowers he had ever seen. He stopped to pick some and made them into a pretty posy. Yan then returned to his sheep and played the magic flute. The sheep began to dance around him. At that moment, the princess

looked out of a palace window
and laughed at the dancing
sheep. Then the scent of the
wonderful posy that Yan had
made reached her.

"Run down to that shepherd
and tell him I want that posy," she
told her maid. So the maid did.

But Yan wouldn't give the
posy to the maid. He said, "Tell
the princess she must come and
ask for the posy herself. And

that she must say please."

The princess thought this was funny. But she wanted the posy, so she went down to him and said, "Please give me that posy." And Yan gave her the posy.

Every day after that, Yan took some flowers from

10

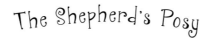

the giant's garden and made a posy for the princess. And every day the princess stood at the palace window and waited for him. Each day she said 'please' when she asked for the posy.

The day came when the princess was to meet all the princes. Yan dressed in his finest royal clothes and went to the palace. The princess thought he was handsome but she wasn't

sure if he was the shepherd.
Before she could speak to Yan,
he rode off on his horse. The
princess told her guards to stop
him, and one grabbed Yan's foot,
but he managed to get away.

The princess wanted to find
out if the shepherd was really
the prince. So she ran to the
field where the sheep were
grazing. As soon as she saw the
shepherd's injured foot she

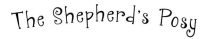

knew he was the prince that her guards had tried to stop. She begged Yan to tell her the truth.

"Please tell me!" said the princess. And because she said 'please' Yan told her that he was really a prince.

The princess was overjoyed, and said that Yan was the prince she wanted to marry. So they were married and lived happily ever after.

The Blacksmith's Daughter

In a wooden house deep in the forest lived a blacksmith and his daughter. The blacksmith worked hard all day shoeing horses, while his daughter kept

the fire, carried water, chopped wood, dug the garden and cooked the meals. Her hands were rough, her face pale with little sleep, and her hair matted with dirt. Even so, men came seeking her hand in marriage. But the girl said, "I won't marry until I find someone I love with all my heart."

One day, the King's messenger came to proclaim that the prince of the kingdom had been cursed by a sorcerer and imprisoned in a cave sealed with three locks.

The King offered a reward of his kingdom's greatest treasure to anyone who could rescue the prince. The young nobles of the land went off to try their luck.

The next day, the blacksmith's daughter put down her tools and said, "Father, if you can manage without me, I've a mind to try to rescue the prince myself."

So she packed a bundle of her tools, and walked through the forest till she came to the cave. The king and queen were there, as was the king's messenger.

The cave had an iron door three feet thick, with three mighty keyholes.

17

In front of it stood three towering pillars, one of flame, one of ice, and one of wax.

"On the top of each pillar," said the king's messenger, "is a key to one of the keyholes. But the wax pillar is too smooth to climb, the ice pillar too slippery, and the fire pillar has killed scores of our best knights."

All day the blacksmith's daughter watched as man after

man tried their luck. Many were hurt, and all were carried away to be tended in the King's tent.

At last it was her turn. "Hmm," she said. "This is work for someone who understands work."

She went into the forest with her axe, gathered bundles of wood and built a huge fire around the base of the ice pillar. Next she dug a channel between the ice pillar and the fire pillar.

She lit the fire and soon had a roaring blaze. Slowly, the ice began to melt and the pillar grew smaller. As the ice melted, the water gathered in the channel and ran down to the pillar of flame. It surged against the pillar and the fires at the bottom died away. The whole pillar collapsed.

As it fell, the key from the top of it shot into the grass where the blacksmith's daughter

found it. At the same moment,
the ice pillar dwindled to a
height where she could reach up
to seize the key from its top.

Only the wax pillar was left.
She shovelled up some hot coals
from the pillar of flames, and
spread them at the base of the
pillar of wax. The heat softened
the wax just enough to allow her
to carve out small holes, like
steps, in its side. Putting her

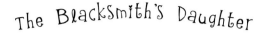

foot into the first hole and
cutting another one for her hand,
she started to climb.

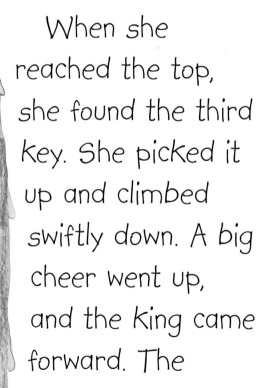

When she
reached the top,
she found the third
key. She picked it
up and climbed
swiftly down. A big
cheer went up,
and the king came
forward. The

22

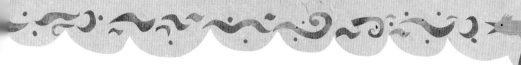

three keys were fitted to the
locks and out came the prince.

His gaze fell on the
blacksmith's daughter. The ice
water had washed the dust
from her hair, the fire had put
colour in her cheeks and the
wax had softened her hands.
The prince could not take his
eyes off her.

"You deserve any reward you
care to claim," said the king.

The Blacksmith's Daughter

"Name it and it shall be yours."

The blacksmith's daughter said simply, "Your majesty offered as a reward his greatest treasure. Is not the prince your greatest treasure?"

The prince smiled at the blacksmith's daughter, the king signalled his approval and the people cheered. So, the pair were married, and they lived happily ever after.

This book belongs to

. . . .

First published in 2018 by Miles Kelly Publishing Ltd
Harding's Barn, Bardfield End Green, Thaxted, Essex, CM6 3PX, UK

2 4 6 8 10 9 7 5 3 1

Publishing Director Belinda Gallagher
Creative Director Jo Cowan
Editorial Director Rosie Neave
Senior Editor Becky Miles
Design Managers Joe Jones, Simon Lee
Image Manager Liberty Newton
Production Elizabeth Collins, Caroline Kelly
Reprographics Stephan Davis, Jennifer Cozens
Assets Lorraine King

ISBN 978-1-78617-489-5

Printed in China

British Library Cataloguing-in-Publication Data
A catalogue record for this book is available from the British Library

Acknowledgements

The publishers would like to thank the following artists who have contributed to this book:
The Bright Agency: Maddie Frost (including decorative frames), Sarah Jennings

Made with paper from a sustainable forest

www.mileskelly.net

The Unhappy Daffodils

The Magic Bracelet

Miles Kelly

The Unhappy Daffodils

Once upon a time, three daffodils grew under a big, old oak tree. They were fed up and bored and decided they wanted a change. A cuckoo had told the daffodils stories about

girls who could run and dance,
and the daffodils wished they
were girls too. Then one day a
fairy heard the daffodils crying,
and she asked them why they
were so unhappy. The daffodils
told the fairy that they wanted
to be girls instead of flowers.

"Very well, my dears, you
shall be girls," said the fairy.
She waved her magic wand over
the three daffodils and in a

twinkle they were gone. In their places stood three pretty girls dressed in soft yellow silk dresses and dancing shoes. The daffodils were shocked, but then they laughed and danced happily around the tree.

They thought they were so clever being girls instead of little flowers that no one really noticed. So they set off to see the world. Suddenly they heard a 'cuck-oo' and saw their old friend the cuckoo. He had good news for them.

"The three princes of Silverland are looking for three brides," he said, and the girls became very excited.

The next day the cuckoo showed the girls the way to the palace. Once they had arrived, the cuckoo told the king that the girls were the Princesses Daffodil from Goldenland. The cuckoo didn't know that there really were three real princesses from Goldenland and that they were on their way to the palace. Everyone thought the daffodil

girls were the real
princesses.

They were invited
to a ball where they
danced with the
princes all night.
Everyone said how
beautiful they
looked.

But the next day the real
princesses of Goldenland
arrived at the palace. The

9

The Unhappy Daffodils

princes couldn't work out who were the real princesses. The only way was to check the girls' feet, as the true princesses had a mark on their big toes. So the princes asked to see all the

princesses' feet to be quite sure who was who. When the princes saw the daffodil girls weren't the real princesses they shouted, "Put them in prison!"

The girls ran from the palace. They ran and ran and ran, not daring to look behind them. Eventually they stopped to rest. And where do you think they were? Why, at their old home under the old oak tree.

The fairy asked, "Well, my dears, do you like being girls?" and there was a twinkle in her eye as she spoke. But the girls were sobbing too much to answer. So the fairy said more kindly, "Will you be happy to be daffodils again?" And they answered, "Yes!"

The fairy waved her magic wand and in a flash the girls

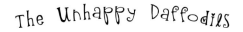

were gone and there were three
beautiful daffodils growing under
the old oak tree once more.
From that day on, no cuckoos
could tell the daffodils to be
anything other than sweet, little
daffodils!

The Magic Bracelet

There was once a princess called Annabel who was sent to live with her uncle in his castle when her parents died. However her uncle was mean, and he made Annabel live in a room at the top of a dusty old tower, away from the rest of her family.

Annabel was frightened all on her own at the top of the tower. One night she heard scratching at her door. Scritch, scratch, scritch.

"Who's there?" said Annabel. There was no answer but she bravely opened the door, and in bounced a friendly, shaggy dog. He leapt on Annabel and licked her face.

"Hello, where did you come from?" laughed Annabel. It was good to have a friend in the lonely tower, and from that night on, the dog, which Annabel called Toby, stayed by her side.

With Toby to keep her company, Annabel felt brave enough to explore the rest of the tower. Many of the rooms were filled with cobwebs and furniture covered in sheets.

Annabel thought every room was the same, until she opened the last door. This room was beautiful, with a soft carpet, pretty flower curtains and a dressing table upon which

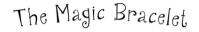

some jewellery sparkled.

Annabel sat at the dressing table and tried on a glittering butterfly brooch, a heart necklace and a gold bracelet. Toby pushed his wet nose against Annabel's leg. He was hungry.

Annabel took off the brooch and the necklace. But when

she tried to take off the bracelet it stuck fast, so she left it on.

Annabel often visited the beautiful room. She would sit at the dressing table, trying on the beautiful jewellery. But however hard she tried, she couldn't take off the gold bracelet.

One evening when Annabel was getting into bed, she called Toby, who always slept on her bed with her. But this particular night, Toby didn't come. "Toby, Toby," called Annabel sadly.

But Toby didn't appear the next night, or the night after that. "I wish I could *see* Toby again," sobbed Annabel.

At that moment, the gold bracelet glowed brightly, and Annabel felt herself flying through the sky. Suddenly she found herself in a garden next to a large cage that was filled with dogs. The dogs had all looked very sad and thin, and Annabel realized they must have been stolen.

"Poor dogs," said Annabel, and she unlocked the cage and set the dogs free. Suddenly, Toby was beside her, barking joyfully, he was so pleased to see her.

"I wish we were home, Toby,"

said Annabel as she gave him a
hug. In a flash, the gold bracelet
glowed, and Annabel and Toby
were back in the tower.
Annabel's uncle was waiting
for her, but he wasn't

22

cross, he was happy to see her home again. "I was worried about you," he said. "Thank you for saving my dog."

Annabel's uncle told her that Toby was his dog, and that he let him stay with Annabel because he knew she needed company. He was very sorry for being mean to Annabel, and invited her to live in the castle with the rest of the family.

The Magic Bracelet

Things were much better when Annabel and Toby moved out of the tower. But Annabel never told her uncle about the gold bracelet. Whenever she wanted to, she would make a wish, the magic bracelet would glow, and Annabel and Toby would go off on an adventure.

This book belongs to

· ·

First published in 2018 by Miles Kelly Publishing Ltd
Harding's Barn, Bardfield End Green, Thaxted, Essex, CM6 3PX, UK

2 4 6 8 10 9 7 5 3 1

Publishing Director Belinda Gallagher
Creative Director Jo Cowan
Editorial Director Rosie Neave
Senior Editor Becky Miles
Design Managers Joe Jones, Simon Lee
Image Manager Liberty Newton
Production Elizabeth Collins, Caroline Kelly
Reprographics Stephan Davis, Jennifer Cozens

ISBN 978-1-78617-494-9

Printed in China

British Library Cataloguing-in-Publication Data
A catalogue record for this book is available from the British Library

Acknowledgements
The publishers would like to thank the following artists who have contributed to this book:
Advocate Art: Natalia Moore
The Bright Agency: Maddie Frost (decorative frames)
Plum Pudding Illustration Agency: Bruno Robert

Made with paper from a sustainable forest

www.mileskelly.net

Snow White and the Seven Dwarfs

A Princess in Disguise

MILES
KELLY

Snow White and the Seven Dwarfs

One winter's day, a baby girl was born to a king and queen. She had skin as white as snow and lips as red as blood, so they named her Snow White.

Sadly, the queen died soon after and the king remarried. His new queen was unkind and vain. She had a magic mirror, to which she would say, "Mirror, mirror, on the wall, who's the fairest of them all?"

"You, O queen are the fairest of them all," the

mirror replied.

Many years later, when Snow White was sixteen, the queen asked the same question, and the mirror replied:

"You, O queen, are very fair – but Snow White is now the fairest of them all."

The queen was furious! She ordered a huntsman to find her stepdaughter and kill her.

The huntsman took Snow

White into the forest, but he could not bring himself to do the wicked deed. Instead, he told Snow White to flee, and went back to the queen, pretending he had carried out her wishes.

In the forest, Snow White ran and ran until evening, when she stumbled across a cottage. She walked up the path and tried the door. To her surprise, it opened. Snow White went inside.

Everything was very small and neat. Against the wall stood seven little beds. Snow White sank down on one and soon fell asleep.

Later that night the owners of the cottage came back – they were seven dwarfs, who had been mining in the mountains for jewels.

When Snow White awoke she explained what had happened. The dwarfs kindly said, "You are welcome to stay here with us."

While the dwarfs went out to work Snow White looked after the cottage. They always warned her to beware of her stepmother.

One day, months later, the magic mirror told the evil queen that Snow White was still alive and living in the forest!

The queen set out to look for her, disguised as an old woman. She took with her an apple that was poisoned on one side. After a while the queen found the dwarfs' cottage and called out to Snow White, "Apples for sale! Delicious, juicy, sweet apples!"

"No, thank you," said Snow White, but the queen wouldn't take no for an answer.

She cut off a piece from the good part of the apple. "Look, I will eat some first," she said. "It is quite safe."

Snow White was hungry, so she took a bite of the apple,

11

from the rosy-red side. Straight away she fell down as if dead!

When the dwarfs came home and found Snow White they wept bitterly. They made a glass coffin for her and, very strangely, she always looked as if she had just fallen asleep.

One day a prince came riding past. He stopped to look at Snow White, but as he leant closer he knocked the coffin. The poisoned apple fell from her mouth and she awoke!

The prince took Snow White to his palace and they soon fell in love. Before long they were married, and the dwarfs were guests of honour at the wedding.

A Princess in Disguise

Once, there was an old woman who lived with her flock of geese in a little mountain cottage. Everyone said she was a witch.

One morning, a handsome young count passed by. He came across the old woman as she was about to carry home two huge baskets of fruit. "Good lady," he said, "let me carry them for you."

"Thank you, sir," she said. The young man heaved the baskets onto his shoulders and, all at once, the woman leapt up onto the baskets and he had to carry her too!

The young count staggered up the mountain reaching the

old woman's cottage when he was just about to drop. She sprang off his back and took the baskets, as her geese ran to meet her. Behind them walked the ugliest girl the count had ever seen. "Go inside, daughter, and put the kettle on," the old woman said.

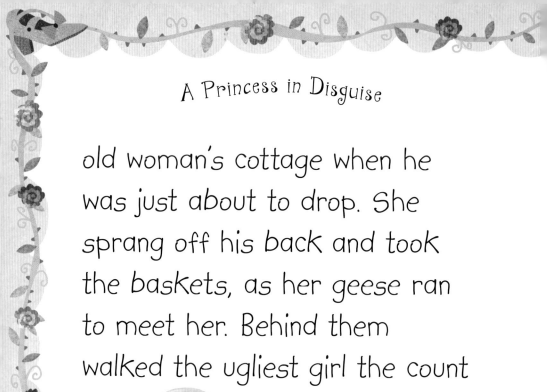

16

The count sank down on a bench, exhausted. Then the old woman said: "Thank you. I have a reward for you." She gave him a small emerald box, saying, "Take great care of it, for it will bring you good fortune."

The count thanked her and set off on his way, but soon got lost in the forest. Three days later, tired and hungry, he found the nearest town and went to the castle, to ask for help. The count was shown into the great hall, where the king and queen were on their thrones. He bowed and offered them the finest thing he had – the emerald box – in return for food and shelter. The queen loved the gift. But on opening the box, she fainted!

When the queen came to, she began to cry, and explained: "I used to have a daughter who

was so beautiful that her eyes
shone like stars, her hair
gleamed like sunbeams and,
when she wept, she cried pearls
instead of tears. My husband
asked her one day, when she was
fifteen, how much she loved him.
She gave a silly reply, saying:
'Food tastes horrid without salt,
so I love you more than salt.'

"The king didn't like that at
all. He was so angry he banished

her from the Kingdom! The next day he was sorry, but no one could find her. We haven't seen her since. But when I opened your emerald box, I saw a pearl inside just like the ones she used to cry! Where did you get it?"

The count told the queen about the old woman. He said he hadn't seen the princess, but the queen wanted to see for herself.

The next day, the count,

queen and King set off for the cottage. The count arrived first. He saw the geese outside, with the old woman's ugly daughter, standing at the well. The girl began to wash herself, and to the count's amazement, she peeled off the skin which covered her face and laid it on

the ground, as if it was a mask.
And then how different she
looked! Her eyes gleamed like
the stars and her golden hair
flowed like sunbeams. The count
thought she was the most
beautiful person he'd ever seen!

The king and queen arrived
and the count told them
everything. They rushed into the
cottage and found the witch
and... the beautiful princess! At

first, the girl thought she was dreaming. Then she sprang up and hugged her parents, who wept with joy.

"Your daughter has a pure heart, yet you threw her out," the old woman scolded. "She has lived here with me in disguise, so no one bothered her, and she has been well looked after. I kept the tears that she cried over you, so now she has a

A Princess in Disguise

fortune in pearls. As my own gift, I give her my cottage." And with that, the old woman disappeared. The cottage walls rattled and a huge cloud of dust flew up. When it cleared, everyone was standing in a fine palace, with servants waiting to do their bidding...

The count and the princess fell in love. They married and lived in the new palace happily ever after.

24

The
Firebird

♥

Rapunzel

Miles Kelly

The Firebird

Many years ago, the king's archer was riding through the forest when he found a shining feather on the ground. It was gold and glittered like a flame. The archer

knew that such a beautiful feather could only be from the firebird, so he took it to the King.

But the King was not happy with just the feather. "A feather is not a gift for a great King!" he said. "Bring me the firebird or I will have you killed!"

In despair, the poor archer left the King. He didn't know how he could find the firebird. But his wise, old horse said, "Ask the

king to scatter a hundred sacks of seeds over the fields." So the archer did and it was done.

The next day, the archer and his horse hid behind a hedge. Suddenly, there was a gust of wind and a huge golden firebird

6

flew into the field. It dropped down and began to eat the seeds.

The archer crept nearer. Then, quick as a flash, he leapt on the firebird and tied it up with strong ropes. He took it to the King.

But the King was still not happy. He locked the firebird in a cage, and this time he said, "Bring me Princess Vassa or I will have you killed!"

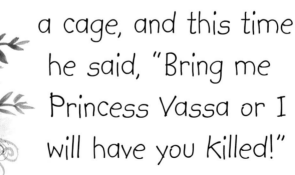

7

Again the archer left the King in despair. But his wise horse said to him, "Ask the King for a golden tent and some delicious food." So the archer asked and it was done.

Then the archer set off on his trusty horse. They boarded a ship and sailed across the sea to the land where Princess Vassa lived.

Once he was there, the archer set up the golden tent and laid out the food. It all looked lovely, and the young archer invited the princess to dine with him.

But the archer had mixed a sleeping potion in the food. As soon as the princess took one bite, she fell asleep. The archer

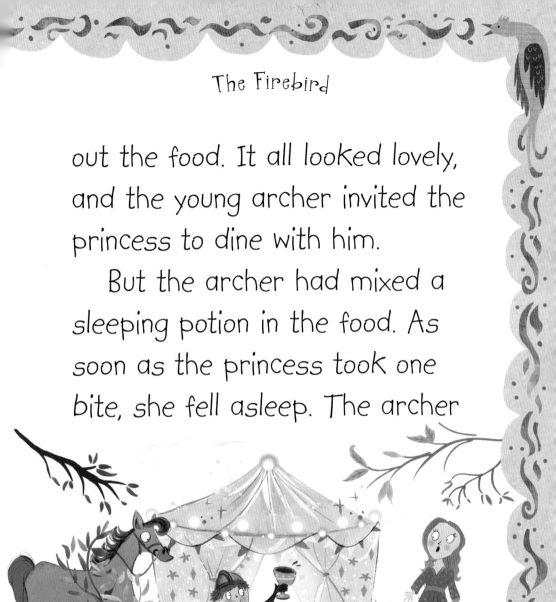

gently placed the princess on his horse and took her to the King.

The King fell in love with the princess and wanted to marry her, but Princess Vassa didn't want to marry the mean King. She didn't tell the King that she had really fallen in love with the Kind and gentle archer. So she said, "I will not marry anyone unless I have my wedding dress. You'll find it locked in a big chest

in the middle of the sea."

Immediately the King called
for the archer. "Bring back that
dress, or I will have you killed!"
he said. So once more the
archer set off on his horse.
They came to the sea where a
great wave crashed on the shore
and hundreds of crabs came out
carrying the chest with Princess
Vassa's wedding dress inside.

The archer took the wedding

dress to the King. He was sad because he had fallen in love with the princess. But the clever princess had a plan. "I won't marry you until you free the firebird," she said to the King. So the King did just that.

Then the firebird swooped down, the princess jumped on its back and they flew into the sky. The King ordered the archer to go after the princess, so he leapt on his horse and chased the firebird across the sea to the land where the princess lived. But he didn't bring her back. Instead the archer and Princess Vassa were married, and lived happily ever after.

Rapunzel

Once, there lived a man and woman who were expecting their first baby. Their cottage overlooked a beautiful garden. However, they never went in the garden for it belonged to a witch.

One morning, the woman was looking into the witch's garden,

when she saw a fresh bed of salad and longed to eat some.

That night, her husband climbed over the wall, grabbed a handful of salad and hurried back to his wife. It was delicious! So, the next night, her husband crept over the wall again. To his horror, there was the witch!

"So, you are the one who stole my salad!" she hissed. Trembling, the man told her about his sick, pregnant wife. "I see," said the witch. "In that case, take all the salad you wish, but you must give me your child when it is born."

The man was heartbroken but knew the witch was powerful. So he promised her what she wanted and fled back home.

Soon the child was born – a baby girl. The witch appeared, picked her up and said: "I will take good care of her." Then

she disappeared...

The witch called the baby Rapunzel. She wanted Rapunzel all to herself, so she raised her in a high tower deep in a forest. The tower had no door or stairs, just a window at the top, so the witch had to magic herself in and out.

Away from the world, Rapunzel grew into a

good, beautiful girl. By the time she was twelve, her hair had grown so long and thick that she could let it out of the window like a rope, for the witch to climb up and down.

One morning, when Rapunzel was eighteen, a prince was riding through the forest when he heard singing. He followed the sound to the tower, for the voice was Rapunzel's. The prince could not find a way in and sank down by a tree, disappointed.

The witch soon arrived and, not noticing the prince, cried out: "Rapunzel! Rapunzel! Let down your hair!" The golden braid came tumbling out of the tower window and the witch climbed up. The prince waited till evening, then hurried to the tower. "Rapunzel! Rapunzel! Let down your hair!" he cried. To his delight, the braid came out of the window and he climbed up.

Rapunzel was terrified! She had never seen anyone but the witch before. However, the prince spoke to her gently and smiled so kindly that she lost her fear.

The couple talked and laughed and, before the sun rose, they had fallen in love. The prince left before the witch arrived but he promised to return that night.

And so he did... and the next night... and every night after that. Each time, he took with him some silk for Rapunzel to weave a long ladder to escape from the tower.

Days went by and the secret ladder grew longer and longer. But one day, while talking to the witch, Rapunzel forgot herself.

"You are so slow to climb – the prince is much quicker!" she said.

The witch was furious! She grabbed a pair of scissors and cut off Rapunzel's braid. Then she magicked the girl far away into an empty desert.

The witch tied the braid to the tower window. When she heard the prince calling, she let down the braid. The prince climbed up – and there was the witch!

"Aha!" she cried. "Now you will never see Rapunzel again!" As the witch began to cast a spell, the prince leapt out of the tower window. He fell into some thorns, which pierced his eyes and left him blind. He stumbled off through the forest, heartbroken.

He wandered the land for a year – until at last he came to the desert where Rapunzel had been banished.

When she saw him she threw
her arms around him, crying
tears of joy. As her tears fell
onto the prince's eyes, they
cleared. He
could see once
more! Finally he
led Rapunzel back
to his kingdom –
where they
lived happily
ever after.

This book
belongs to

. . . .

First published in 2018 by Miles Kelly Publishing Ltd
Harding's Barn, Bardfield End Green, Thaxted, Essex, CM6 3PX, UK

Copyright © Miles Kelly Publishing Ltd 2018

2 4 6 8 10 9 7 5 3 1

Publishing Director Belinda Gallagher
Creative Director Jo Cowan
Editorial Director Rosie Neave
Senior Editor Becky Miles
Design Managers Joe Jones, Simon Lee
Image Manager Liberty Newton
Production Elizabeth Collins, Caroline Kelly
Reprographics Stephan Davis, Jennifer Cozens
Assets Lorraine King

ISBN 978-1-78617-492-5

Printed in China

British Library Cataloguing-in-Publication Data
A catalogue record for this book is available from the British Library

Acknowledgements

The publishers would like to thank the following artists who have contributed to this book:
The Bright Agency: Mélanie Florian, Maddie Frost (decorative frames), Maxine Lee

Made with paper from a sustainable forest

www.mileskelly.net

King Grisly-beard

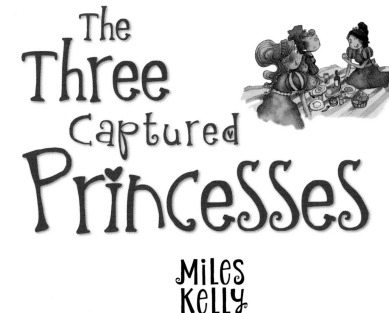

♥

The Three Captured Princesses

MILES
KELLY

King Grisly-beard

There was once a king who had a beautiful daughter. But the princess was so proud that not one of the princes who came to ask her to marry him was good enough for her.

King Grisly-beard

One day the King invited all the princes who wanted to marry his daughter to a grand feast. But the princess said something mean to every man.

The first man was too fat. "He's as round as a tub," she said. The next man was too tall. "What a tree!" she said. The third man was too short and the fourth was too pale, and so she made a joke about every man.

She also laughed at a king who attended. "His beard is like a mop and he should be called Grisly-beard!" she said. And so the visiting king got the name of King Grisly-beard.

The princess's father was angry at her rudeness, as these men were their

guests. So he said that the princess had to marry the next man who knocked at the palace gate. Two days later a fiddler came knocking and the king invited him in and said he could marry the princess. The princess begged her father to change his mind, but he refused.

So the fiddler and the princess were married. The fiddler led the princess through

a wood and she wondered who it belonged to. The fiddler told her that it belonged to King Grisly-beard, and the princess replied, "If only I had married King Grisly-beard!"

Next the fiddler took the princess through beautiful meadows filled with wildflowers. She asked the fiddler who the meadows belonged to, and again he said they belonged to King

Grisly-beard. The princess sighed and said, "If only I had married King Grisly-beard!"

Eventually they arrived at a tiny cottage and the fiddler said

to the princess, "This is your new home, it is up to you to keep it clean and tidy." The unhappy princess also had to do all the cooking and washing too, but she wasn't very good at any of these things.

So the fiddler sent the princess to the nearest market to try to sell pots and pans instead. But she wasn't very good at that either, and didn't sell a thing. The fiddler said, "Perhaps you could try working in the kitchen at the palace of King Grisly-beard." So the princess got a job working as a maid in the palace kitchens.

   After a while the princess heard that the king was getting married. This made her sad as she remembered

that she was really a princess,
but she knew her pride had
brought her to where she
was now.

Suddenly, someone walked
into the kitchen and turned to
the princess. He asked her to
dance. The princess realized
that it was King Grisly-beard
himself. She thought he was
making fun of her, and everyone
laughed at the princess dressed

in maid's clothes. The princess ran to the door, but King Grisly-beard stopped her from leaving.

"I am the fiddler who married you. I pretended to be a fiddler to teach you a lesson about your silly pride."

So the princess was dressed in her most beautiful clothes, and a big feast was held for her and King Grisly-beard, and they lived happily ever after.

The Three Captured Princesses

There was once a King and queen who had three beautiful daughters, and they lived to make the girls happy. One day the princesses wished

to have a picnic in the country.
So the royal family took their
carriage to a pretty spot. They
ate a delicious picnic and then
the princesses said to their
parents, "Now we should like to
wander about the woods a little,
but when you want to go home,

just call to us." And they ran off.

Meanwhile the king and queen sat lazily among the heather. After a while they decided it was time to go home. They called to the princesses but no one replied.

They searched the wood, but found no trace of the girls. The queen wept all the way home, and the king decreed that whoever should bring back his daughters would have one of them to marry.

Living in the palace was a faithful servant called Bensurdatu, and when he saw how sad the king was he said, "Your majesty, let me seek your daughters."

Bensurdatu set out. He rode for many miles until he saw a light in the window of a tiny hut.

"Who goes there?" asked a voice, as he knocked at the door.

"Please can you give me shelter," said Bensurdatu, "I have

lost my way."

The door was opened by an old woman who asked his business.

"I have a hard task," he replied, "I have to find the princesses and bring them home! Tell me, if you know where they are, my good woman," he begged, "for with them lies all our happiness."

"Even if I were to tell you," she answered, "you could not rescue them. Ogres guard them at the

bottom of
a deep river."
Bensurdatu thanked her and
said he would try his luck. Next
morning he woke early
and set off for the
river, borrowing the
old woman's bucket and
chain from her well.
When he came
to the riverbank
he let himself

down into the river. Terrible thunder rose up around him but he bravely went on.

He wandered for a time, then found himself in a large, light hall, and in the middle sat the eldest princess. In front of her lay a huge ogre, fast asleep. The princess saw Bensurdatu and asked how he came to be there.

In answer he drew his sword, and killed the ogre. The

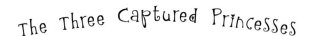

princess's heart leapt! She put a golden crown on Bensurdatu's head, and called him her rescuer.

"Show me where your sisters are," he said. The princess led him into another hall, where one of her sisters was guarded by a second sleeping ogre. When the second princess saw them, she told them to hide, for the ogre was waking up.

"I smell man's flesh!" it said.

"How could any man get down here?" asked the princess. "Go to sleep again." As soon as the ogre closed its eyes, Bensurdatu ran out and struck a blow that killed him. The princess then placed her crown in Bensurdatu's hand.

"Now show me where your youngest sister is," said he.

The princesses opened another door, and Bensurdatu

stepped into a third hall. There stood the youngest sister, guarded by a horrible serpent with seven heads! As Bensurdatu stepped forward it twisted its heads towards him, and tried to snatch him. But Bensurdatu drew his sword and swung it about, until the serpent was no more. He rushed to the princess and she wept for joy and embraced him. She placed her golden crown in his hand.

The king and queen were overjoyed when they saw their daughters once more. A wedding feast was ordered for the marriage of Bensurdatu and the youngest princess – and they lived happily ever after.

This book
belongs to

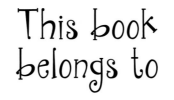

. . . .

First published in 2018 by Miles Kelly Publishing Ltd
Harding's Barn, Bardfield End Green, Thaxted, Essex, CM6 3PX, UK

Copyright © Miles Kelly Publishing Ltd 2018

2 4 6 8 10 9 7 5 3 1

Publishing Director Belinda Gallagher
Creative Director Jo Cowan
Editorial Director Rosie Neave
Senior Editor Becky Miles
Design Managers Joe Jones, Simon Lee
Image Manager Liberty Newton
Production Elizabeth Collins, Caroline Kelly
Reprographics Stephan Davis, Jennifer Cozens
Assets Lorraine King

ISBN 978-1-78617-484-0

Printed in China

British Library Cataloguing-in-Publication Data
A catalogue record for this book is available from the British Library

Acknowledgements

The publishers would like to thank the following artists who have contributed to this book:
The Bright Agency: Maddie Frost (decorative frames), Louise Wright

Made with paper from a sustainable forest

www.mileskelly.net

The Giant who Counted Carrots

The Frog Princess

MILES KELLY

The Giant who Counted Carrots

Once upon a time there was a giant who lived beneath the mountains. One morning he decided to take a walk above the mountains. As he did, he saw a beautiful princess sitting beside a rock pool. The giant fell in love with the princess, and decided to try to win her heart. He changed the rocks into glittering jewels and put a sparkling fountain in the middle of the pool.

The princess wanted more than anything to paddle in the beautiful rock pool. But as soon as she dipped her bare feet in the water, she was dragged

under. Down, down, down she sank...and then she was gone!

The princess had been dragged beneath the mountains to the giant's magical palace. But the giant didn't want to hurt the princess. He showed her

all round his palace and
gardens, where he grew rows
and rows of tasty vegetables.

So the princess stayed with
the giant. But the splendid
palace and gardens were not
enough to put a smile on the
princess's face. This was
because she was missing her
friends and family, but she
didn't tell the giant. The giant
saw that the princess was

The Giant who Counted Carrots

unhappy, and then he
remembered his magic wand.
Whatever it touched would turn
into anything he
wished for. So
the giant gave the
wand to the princess.
She wished for her
little dog Benny,
and her friends.
For a while the princess was
happy again, but the magic

didn't last for long and her pet and friends soon disappeared.

Meanwhile a young prince, who had won the heart of the princess back home, wandered over the mountains looking for his love. At the castle, the clever princess had thought up a plan to escape. She pretended to the giant that she was in love with him, and one day she said, "How can I be sure you love me?"

The Giant who Counted Carrots

The giant replied, "Give me a test, my love." So the princess told the giant to go and count all of the carrots in his field. At once, the giant rushed off to do as the princess asked and show his love for her.

But as soon as he had gone, the princess used the magic wand to turn a potato into a horse. She leapt on the horse's back and galloped out from

The Giant who Counted Carrots

under the mountains straight into the arms of her prince. And she left the giant still counting carrots in the garden!

The Frog Princess

Long ago, it was time for the King's youngest son to marry. The King said, "Shoot this arrow and you will meet your wife where it lands."

But the prince's arrow landed

in a swamp beside a frog. Young Prince Ivan was not happy. "How can I marry a frog?" he asked, but the King wouldn't change his mind. So the prince married the frog and they lived in a castle next to the swamp.

The King was getting old and he was thinking

about which son to give his
palace to. One day he set a test
and asked his sons to bring
their wives to the palace. Prince
Ivan was worried. He didn't want
people to laugh at his Frog
Princess. But his wife said,
"Don't worry, everything will
be fine."

That night when the prince
went to bed he pretended to fall
asleep. He opened one eye and

saw his wife take off her frog skin and change into a young lady. She was so beautiful that he fell in love with her at once.

The next morning the prince said nothing to his wife about what he'd seen. He went to the palace alone and saw that his brothers were there with their grand wives. Suddenly, the palace doors opened and the most beautiful princess walked in. Prince Ivan said to the King, "This is my dear Frog Princess."

Prince Ivan felt sure that the King would give his palace to him. To make sure, he ran home and threw his wife's frog skin into the fire. At this there was a clap of thunder and his wife stood before him.

16

"Why did you burn my frog skin?" she cried. "Now I must leave you forever!" Then she disappeared.

Prince Ivan set off to find his wife. On his way he met an old man who gave him a ball. "Roll this ball and it will show you the way," said the man. Next the prince met a bear, which he was going to eat for his dinner. But the bear begged the prince to let it live. The prince felt sorry for the bear so he agreed, and they set off together after the ball.

Then a duck flew overhead and the prince took aim with a bow and arrow. But the duck begged the prince to let it live. The prince took pity on the duck too, and set off after the ball with the bear and the duck.

After a while the prince and his friends came to a river. A

fish leapt out of the water onto the bank. "At last I shall have a good meal," said the prince. But the fish begged to be thrown back into the water. The prince felt sorry for the fish so he did as it asked.

The Frog Princess

A little further on, the prince met an old woman. She told him that a witch had taken his wife prisoner and that he must get a special needle to kill the witch and free his wife. This needle was inside an egg that was in a nest on top of a tree.

The prince and his friends set off to look for the tree, which they found quite easily. However, the trunk of the tree

was so smooth that when Prince
Ivan tried to climb it, he kept
slipping down. The bear said "I
can help you," and he shook the
tree so hard that the nest fell

from its branches. But there
was a bird sitting on the nest,
and it flew off with the egg
grasped in its feet.

Then the duck said, "I can
help you," and it flew after the
bird. The bird was so scared of
the duck that it dropped the
egg into the river below. The
prince cried, "My wife is lost
forever! For how can I get the
egg from the river?"

Suddenly
the fish that
the prince had
thrown back
into the river
appeared. It had the egg in its
mouth as it swam to the prince.
The prince quickly broke the
egg and took out the needle.

At this, a witch suddenly
appeared, and ran towards the
prince, but when she set eyes on

the needle she disappeared in a puff of smoke and was never seen again. The spell was broken and the frog princess was free. Prince Ivan went home to find his beautiful wife had returned, and that the King had built them a palace of their own, which was nowhere near the swamp!

Prince
Hyacinth
and the
Dear Little
Princess

♥

A
Troublesome
Dragon

Miles Kelly

Prince Hyacinth and the Dear Little Princess

There was once a fairy who said to a king, "You will have a son with a big nose, and your son will never be truly happy until he discovers that his nose is big."

4

Soon after this, the fairy's spell came true. The King did indeed have a son, who was named Prince Hyacinth, and he did have a big nose.

However the King didn't want his son to feel self-conscious about his nose. He ordered that only people with big noses were allowed to be in the prince's company, and that no one could say anything about big noses in

front of him.
Because of this,
the prince
wasn't the
slightest bit
bothered by
his nose!
One day,
when Prince
Hyacinth
was grown
up, his

6

father said he should marry. The prince liked the look of a neighbouring princess called the Dear Little Princess, even though she had a tiny nose, so he paid her a visit and asked her to marry him. But as he bent down to kiss her hand, the princess disappeared. Prince Hyacinth leapt on his horse and went to look for her.

He rode all day, until he came

across a cave where a fairy lived. The fairy and the prince looked at each other and laughed. "What a funny nose!" they both cried. The fairy thought the prince's nose was too big, and the prince thought the fairy's nose was too small.

The prince carried on his search for the princess. But everyone laughed at him. He

Prince Hyacinth and the Dear Little Princess

didn't know why, as he couldn't
see that his nose was that big.

Then at last the prince found
the Dear Little Princess locked
inside a palace made of glass.
She held her hand out of the
window for the prince to kiss.
But he couldn't reach her, as his
nose got in the way. He cried,
"My nose must be too big!"

At last the prince knew that
he had a big nose! The spell

that the fairy had placed on him was broken and the glass palace shattered into pieces. The princess was free, and she married Prince Hyacinth, who was happy at last.

A Troublesome Dragon

Once upon a time in a faraway land a king asked his advisors, "Who can get rid of the dragon that's eating our food and scaring my people?"

The king's daughter, Princess

Iris, said, "I'll get rid of the dragon, father."

But the King replied, "Don't you worry about the dragon my dear. My brave Knights will help to solve this problem."

The first Knight to step forward to help was called Sir Tickle. He got his name from a long blue feather that hung from his helmet and tickled his face. Everyone Knows that dragons

hate water, so Sir Tickle set off
with a long hose to the dragon's
cave, which was on a nearby hill.
But the dragon saw Sir Tickle
coming. He pressed a button
on his magic belt and a
cape covered him up.

Sir Tickle shouted
to a servant, "Turn on
the tap!" and water
poured over the
dragon. But the

cape kept him dry. Sir Tickle
went back to the King and told
him that the dragon was too
clever for him.

The next knight to try and
get rid of the dragon was
Sir Bright. He liked to wear
bright clothes – so he was the
perfect knight to face the
dragon, as dragons hate bright
colours, especially red. Sir Bright
dressed from head to toe in

red, and even put a red coat on his horse.

When the clever dragon saw Sir Bright trotting boldly towards him on his horse, again he pressed a button on his magic belt. This time a pair of special glasses popped over his eyes. Even when Sir Bright and his horse stood right in front of the dragon wearing their bright red clothes, he wasn't bothered

A Troublesome Dragon

at all. He found it very funny and laughed really hard! Sir Bright went back to the King and said the dragon was too wise.

Secretly, Princess Iris had followed each knight to the dragon's cave and she noticed that the dragon always wore a belt. The clever princess guessed that the belt was magic, and that this helped the dragon to stop the knights.

A Troublesome Dragon

One night, Princess Iris crept out of the palace to the dragon's cave. The dragon was snoring loudly, and the princess carefully tiptoed around him. The dragon's magic belt was lying on the floor. Princess Iris dragged the belt out of the cave – it was too heavy for her to carry. She pulled it into a field and buried it.

Then Princess Iris went back

to the palace, and got the hose and put on a red cape. Day was breaking and the dragon was waking up. He fumbled around his cave for his magic belt but it wasn't there. Someone had stolen it! The dragon was very angry. He stormed out of his cave to look for the thief, just as Princess Iris arrived. Her bright red cape hurt the dragon's eyes. Suddenly the princess sprayed water all over the dragon. He was drenched! Not only did the dragon hate bright colours, he hated being wet, too.

A Troublesome Dragon

"I'm not staying here anymore!" he growled as he flapped his wings and flew off in a huff.

And from that day on, if the king needed any help he always asked clever Princess Iris first.

This book
belongs to

. . . .

First published in 2018 by Miles Kelly Publishing Ltd
Harding's Barn, Bardfield End Green, Thaxted, Essex, CM6 3PX, UK

2 4 6 8 10 9 7 5 3 1

Publishing Director Belinda Gallagher
Creative Director Jo Cowan
Editorial Director Rosie Neave
Senior Editor Becky Miles
Design Managers Joe Jones, Simon Lee
Image Manager Liberty Newton
Production Elizabeth Collins, Caroline Kelly
Reprographics Stephan Davis, Jennifer Cozens
Assets Lorraine King

ISBN 978-1-78617-475-8

Printed in China

British Library Cataloguing-in-Publication Data
A catalogue record for this book is available from the British Library

Acknowledgements

The publishers would like to thank the following artists who have contributed to this book:
The Bright Agency: Maddie Frost (decorative frames), Clair Rossiter, Louise Wright

Made with paper from a sustainable forest

www.mileskelly.net

The Princess and the Hare

♥

The Goose Girl

MILES KELLY

The Princess and the Hare

There was once a queen who wanted a child. One day the queen said to the sun, "Please sun, send me a little girl. When she is twelve years old, I will give her back to you."

Soon after this, the Sun sent the queen a little girl, whom she called Letiko. The queen loved her little princess dearly. When Letiko was twelve, the sun said to her one day, "Tell your mother to remember what she said to me." Letiko went home and told the queen this.

The queen was scared that the sun would come to take her daughter away. She shut all the

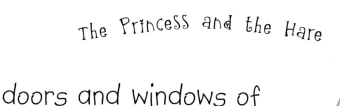

doors and windows of
the palace and hid
Letiko. But she forgot
to close up the keyhole.
The sun shone through the
keyhole and took Letiko
away. She went to live with
the sun to do his work.

Letiko was unhappy,
as she missed her
mother. One day the sun
heard Letiko crying. This

made him sad, so he asked two hares to take Letiko home.

The hares and Letiko set off. But before long, the hares grew hungry, and asked Letiko to hide in a tree while they ate.

"Dear Letiko, wait in this tree until we've finished eating some grass." So Letiko climbed the tree and the hares went off to find some grass.

A witch had seen Letiko climb the tree. She said, "Letiko, Letiko, come down from the tree and look at my beautiful shoes."

But Princess Letiko replied, "My shoes are more beautiful than your shoes. Go away!"

So then the witch said, "Letiko, Letiko, come down from the tree and look at my fine apron."

But brave Letiko replied, "My apron is finer than your apron. Go away!"

The witch went away, but returned with an axe and said, "If you will not come down, I will cut down the tree!"

Letiko cried, "Chop down the tree, then!" So the witch chopped at the tree, but she couldn't cut it down.

When the witch had gone,

Letiko cried, "Little hares! Come back!" The hares heard Letiko and ran back as fast as they could. Letiko came down from the tree and told them about the witch. They hurried on to the palace. But the witch hadn't gone far, and was soon chasing after them.

When Letiko was nearly at the palace, the queen's

dog recognized her. It
rushed out and cried, "Bow
wow! Letiko is home!"
Then the queen's cat also
saw Letiko and cried, "Meow,
Meow! Letiko is home!"
But the queen didn't
believe them and said,
"Be quiet!"
Letiko and the hares

ran into the the palace, but the witch was close behind them. She grabbed the tail of one hare before it got inside, and pulled the tail off before the door was slammed in her face.

The queen saw the little hare without a tail and said, "Dear hare, because you have brought my Letiko home, I will give you a silver tail in place of the tail you've lost." So she did, and the

hare with the silver tail and the other hare, his best friend, lived happily ever after with Princess Letiko.

The Goose Girl

Once upon a time there was a beautiful princess. When she grew up she was expected to marry a prince who lived in a faraway land. So the princess set off for the prince's palace with her maid. She rode a talking horse called Falada, given to her by a good fairy.

On the way, the princess became thirsty so she asked her maid for a drink. But the maid replied, "Get it yourself!" The princess was surprised and a little afraid. They rode on, but the sun was so hot that the princess was soon thirsty again. Once more the princess asked her maid for a drink, but again she refused to get one.

Then the maid said, "I will ride Falada and you will ride my horse." The princess was too scared to say no. She also had to give the maid her royal clothes, and put on the maid's dirty clothes.

At last they reached the prince's palace, and the maid said she

would make sure the princess
went to prison if she told anyone
what had happened. But Falada
had seen everything.

The prince was happy to see
the princess – he didn't know
that it was the maid dressed
in the princess's clothes. The
real princess was sent to
look after the King's geese
with a boy called Conrad.
The maid was worried

that Falada would tell the prince she wasn't really the princess. So she said to him, "The horse I rode here was very wild, I want you to set it free." The prince was surprised but he didn't want to upset her. So poor Falada was banished from the kingdom. The real princess wept when she heard what had happened.

The next day, the real

princess and Conrad went to tend the King's geese. Falada was waiting for them. The princess cried, "Oh Falada! Look at you, all alone!"

And Falada replied, "Dear princess, if your mother knew what had happened her heart would be broken."

Conrad and the princess took the geese into a field, and the princess stopped to comb her hair. Conrad wanted a strand of her lovely hair but the princess said, "Blow wind, blow! Blow Conrad's hat! Go!" At once a

gust of wind blew Conrad's hat away and he had to chase after it. When he returned, the princess had tied her hair back, and Conrad was angry and would not speak to her.

The next day the same thing happened, and the day after that. At the end of the third day, Conrad spoke to the King.

"I cannot look after the geese with that girl anymore as she teases me." Conrad told the King what happened, but the King told him to go out again the next day.

This time the King hid behind the gate. He heard what the real princess said to Falada, and what Falada replied. He saw how the princess's hair glittered in the sun, and he heard her tell the wind to blow Conrad's hat away. When she returned that evening the King asked her why she said those things to the horse.

"I cannot tell you," she wept. But the King begged her to tell him the truth, so she told him the whole story.

The King was very angry when he heard what had happened. He told his servants to bring the princess her royal clothes. She looked beautiful! Then he told his son that the lady he thought was a princess was really a maid. The maid was sent far away and the prince fell in love with the real princess, and they were married. The good fairy visited and reunited Falada with the princess, and they all lived happily ever after.

This book
belongs to

. . . .

First published in 2018 by Miles Kelly Publishing Ltd
Harding's Barn, Bardfield End Green, Thaxted, Essex, CM6 3PX, UK

2 4 6 8 10 9 7 5 3 1

Publishing Director Belinda Gallagher
Creative Director Jo Cowan
Editorial Director Rosie Neave
Senior Editor Becky Miles
Design Managers Joe Jones, Simon Lee
Image Manager Liberty Newton
Production Elizabeth Collins, Caroline Kelly
Reprographics Stephan Davis, Jennifer Cozens
Assets Lorraine King

ISBN 978-1-78617-487-1

Printed in China

British Library Cataloguing-in-Publication Data
A catalogue record for this book is available from the British Library

Acknowledgements

The publishers would like to thank the following artists who have contributed to this book:
Advocate Art: Natalia Moore
The Bright Agency: Maddie Frost (decorative frames), Louise Wright

Made with paper from a sustainable forest

www.mileskelly.net

The Bamboo Cutter and the Moon Child

The Stubborn Princess

MILES KELLY

The Bamboo Cutter and the Moon Child

A long time ago there lived an old woodcutter and his wife. They were sad because they never had any children.

One morning the woodcutter was chopping bamboo when a

bright light shone out of one of the stems. Inside, the woodcutter found a beautiful, tiny girl. He said, "You are meant to be my child." And he took the girl home, to care for with his wife.

They called the young girl

Princess Moonlight. Everyone said she was beautiful and when she grew up many men wanted to marry her.

One day, five knights came to the house to see Princess Moonlight. They had travelled a long way and waited for days outside the house. Her father felt sorry for the knights and asked his daughter to see them. But clever Princess Moonlight said that she knew nothing about them and that she wanted to give the knights a test before meeting them.

So the princess asked each knight to find something. The first knight had to find a special stone bowl from India. But he didn't want to travel all the way to India, so he found another stone bowl, wrapped it in gold cloth and sent it to the princess.

But when the princess unwrapped the bowl, it didn't shine. The clever princess knew it was not the special bowl she had asked for.

The second knight had to get a branch from a gold and silver tree that grew up a mountain, far away across the sea. The knight set off but his journey across the sea was hard and he soon gave up. So he asked some jewellers to make him a gold and silver branch. The princess looked at the branch and knew it was not the one she had asked for.

The princess told the third knight to go to China to find the fire rat and send its skin to her. But the knight didn't go to

China. Instead he paid a friend who lived in China to send him the skin of a fire rat. The friend took the money but sent a different animal's skin instead. The princess knew that the skin of the real fire rat would not burn so she

10

threw the skin into the fire. The skin burnt at once and the princess knew the knight had tried to trick her.

The fourth knight had to find a dragon with a magic stone. The knight was lazy, so he told his servants to look for the dragon. But after a year his servants couldn't find it, so the knight gave up his search.

The princess told the fifth

11

knight to find a bird with a special shell in its tummy. The fifth knight was lazy like all the others, and he soon gave up his search, too. All the knights, and many after that, were sent home for trying to trick the clever princess.

Then one day, the woodcutter found his daughter crying and asked her what was wrong. She said, "I have come from the moon and soon I have to go back to the moon." The princess was sad that she had to leave the woodcutter and his wife.

The woodcutter didn't want his daughter to go, either. So he told everyone in the house to watch over the princess at night and make sure that no one took her away. Even the King heard and sent his soldiers to guard Princess Moonlight.

But one night a cloud came
down from the moon. A grand
king was in the cloud and said

he had come to take Princess Moonlight home. The princess knew it was time to go back, so she stepped into the cloud. She was sad to leave the woodcutter and his wife, and said to them, "Thank you for taking good care of me. Think of me when you look up at the moon."

The Stubborn Princess

There was once a princess who ate nothing but ice cream. In fact, ever since Princess Uma was a baby she had turned her nose up at

anything but ice cream. The
king and queen tried
to get her to eat
other food but
each time they
tried, Princess
Uma would shout,
"Give me some
ice cream!"
The king and
queen didn't know
what to do, so

17

they sent out a message to everyone in the land: "We'll give a thousand gold coins to anyone who can get our daughter to eat anything other than ice cream." So people queued up at the palace to try to tempt Princess Uma to eat something else.

First to try was Prince Flatter. He made the princess a delicious casserole with chicken, potatoes, mushrooms and carrots. He dished it up in a gold bowl with a gold spoon and placed it before Princess Uma. But the princess took one look at it and shouted, "Give me some ice cream!" So Prince Flatter quickly left the palace with his casserole.

Next to try was Prince Smooth, who was very clever. He had prepared a scrumptious fruit salad made with fresh blueberries, grapes, strawberries and bananas, and then he put a dollop of tasty ice cream on the

top. But the princess wasn't fooled and she shouted, "Give me only ice cream!" So Prince Smooth also ran out of the palace.

Lastly, Prince Perfect came to the palace, and he presented the princess with a large bowl of... ice cream! Princess Uma greedily ate all the ice cream. Then Prince Perfect gave her some more ice cream, which she also ate. And some more ice cream, and some more, and so it went on into the night.

Every time Princess Uma finished eating a bowl of ice cream, Prince Perfect gave her another bowl. Then at last, when Prince Perfect gave Princess

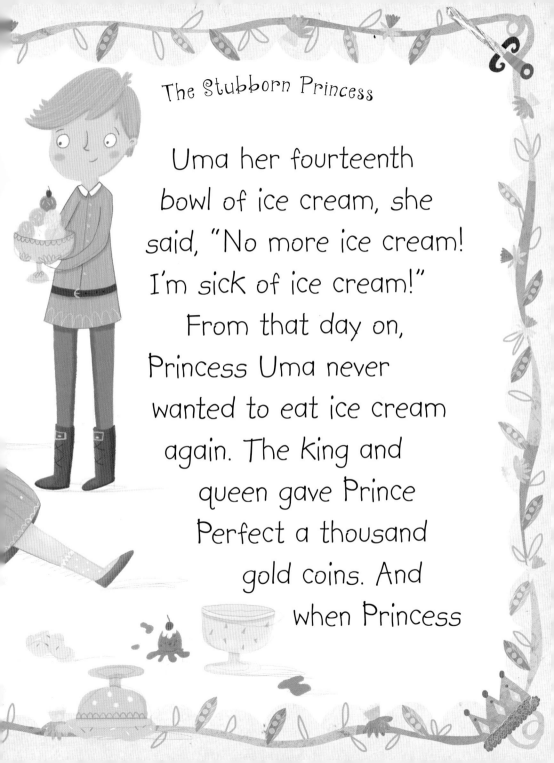

The Stubborn Princess

Uma her fourteenth bowl of ice cream, she said, "No more ice cream! I'm sick of ice cream!"

From that day on, Princess Uma never wanted to eat ice cream again. The King and queen gave Prince Perfect a thousand gold coins. And when Princess

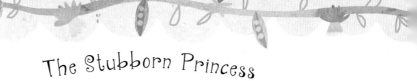

Uma grew up, she and Prince Perfect were married and they lived happily ever after.

This book belongs to

. . . .

First published in 2018 by Miles Kelly Publishing Ltd
Harding's Barn, Bardfield End Green, Thaxted, Essex, CM6 3PX, UK

2 4 6 8 10 9 7 5 3 1

Publishing Director Belinda Gallagher
Creative Director Jo Cowan
Editorial Director Rosie Neave
Senior Editor Becky Miles
Design Managers Joe Jones, Simon Lee
Image Manager Liberty Newton
Production Elizabeth Collins, Caroline Kelly
Reprographics Stephan Davis, Jennifer Cozens
Assets Lorraine King

ISBN 978-1-78617-480-2

Printed in China

British Library Cataloguing-in-Publication Data
A catalogue record for this book is available from the British Library

Acknowledgements

The publishers would like to thank the following artists who have contributed to this book:
The Bright Agency: Maddie Frost (including decorative frames), Sarah Jennings

Made with paper from a sustainable forest

www.mileskelly.net

The Red Slippers

♥

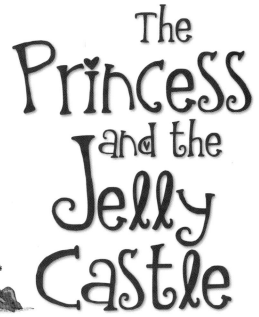

The Princess and the Jelly Castle

MiLeS KeLLY

The Red Slippers

Rosy-red was a sweet little girl, with beautiful brown eyes, soft pink cheeks and dark hair. Sadly her mother died the day Rosy-red was born so the little girl was cared for by her

grandmother, who loved her dearly. On her first birthday Rosy-red's father gave her some red slippers. As Rosy-red's feet grew, her red slippers got bigger too, so they always fitted her. No one knew that the slippers were magic.

One day when Rosy-red returned home from a walk in the woods, she found that her grandmother had gone. In the

house were three strangers.
  "Who are you?" asked
Rosy-Red.

The Red Slippers

"I am your new mother," said one, "and these are your new sisters." Rosy-red's father had married again and his new wife had sent her grandmother away.

Rosy-red's new mother was mean to her. She made her fetch water from the well and carry the heavy bucket all the way home. Her sisters often shouted at her too. Rosy-red was sad, so she didn't wear her red slippers anymore.

Then one day, as Rosy-red lowered the bucket into the well, she sang, "Swing and sweep and don't stop until you come back up to the top."

A genie was sleeping at the bottom of the well and Rosy-red's song woke him. The genie loved her sweet song so much that he dropped some precious jewels into the bucket.

The Red Slippers

Rosy-red thought, 'If I give these jewels to my sisters maybe they will be kinder to me.' So she handed the jewels to her sisters and told them all about what happened at the well. But the sisters weren't happy, and they snatched the jewels and the bucket from Rosy-red.

The sisters ran to the well and as they lowered the bucket

they sang Rosy-red's song. But the genie didn't like their croaky voices, so he filled their bucket with toads and frogs.

The sisters were angry and threw Rosy-red out of the house. She just had time to put on her red

The Red Slippers

slippers, then she ran away into the woods.

After a while it began to get dark and Rosy-red was frightened. She saw a light in a cave, and an old woman invited her inside. It was Rosy-red's grandmother!

Rosy-red was so tired that she soon fell asleep. When she awoke, she found that one of her red slippers was missing. "I must go and look for it," said Rosy-Red.

"You can't do that, a storm is raging," said her grandmother. So Rosy-red went back to sleep.

A little while later, Rosy-red was woken by a man's voice. The man had found a red slipper and he asked Rosy-red's grandmother if she knew who it belonged to. But grandmother

was afraid that Rosy-red's stepsisters had sent him to find her. So she said she didn't know, and the strange man left.

The next day the man called again. He said, "I am a prince. I must find who this shoe belongs to." So Rosy-red bravely stepped out of her hiding place. She was wearing her one red slipper. The prince put the other red slipper on Rosy-red's bare

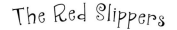

The Red Slippers

foot. "Let us get to know each other. If you like me, we will get married and you will be my princess," said the prince.

The Red Slippers

So Rosy-red left the cave with her grandmother and the prince. She spent many happy days living in the prince's palace and soon they were married. And from then on she always wore her magical red slippers.

The Princess and the Jelly Castle

Once upon a time there was a shy princess called Daisy who was scared of most things. So you can imagine how worried Princess Daisy was when the king and queen told her they were giving her a birthday party, and lots of other young princes and princesses were invited.

On the day of her party Daisy hid upstairs in her bedroom. She was too scared to meet her guests. The queen held Daisy's hand and they walked downstairs. Daisy looked beautiful in her sparkly purple dress and she wore a little purple and gold crown. But all the way to the garden, Daisy looked down at the ground, as she was too frightened to look up. "You're doing great," whispered her mother.

Fairy lights were hung around the garden and all the royal children wore their best clothes. By the pond was the biggest jelly castle you've ever seen!

"Come and play Pin the Tail on the Dragon," said Princess

Candy to Daisy. So Daisy shyly followed. Candy covered Daisy's eyes with a scarf, then spun her around. Daisy wasn't very good at the game and pinned the tail on the wrong end of the dragon. She thought the other children must be laughing at her and her face turned bright red.

Next Daisy tried the Golden Egg and Spoon Race. But she dropped the egg at the start and quickly ran and hid behind the King. "I'm not very good at any of the games," she said.

"It doesn't matter. Just try your best," said the King.

Then Prince Theo asked Daisy to have a race with him. But Daisy's knees were shaking and she was too scared to move. Just at that moment she looked across the garden and saw Prince Butterfingers carrying a plate of sausages. He wasn't looking where he was going and he was walking towards the deep pond – and he couldn't swim!

Without thinking, Daisy ran as fast as she could across the garden and pushed Prince Butterfingers out of the way, just in time! Everyone at the party stopped talking and looked at Daisy and Prince

Butterfingers. They had both
fallen in the jelly castle
and were covered from
head to toe in sticky
pink jelly! Then
Daisy looked at
Prince Butterfingers,
and they both burst
out laughing.

Prince Theo ran
up to Daisy and
said, "You won

23

the race!" and he gave Daisy a rosette. Brave Princess Daisy had saved Prince Butterfingers and she had also won a race. She had quite forgotten her shyness. This was the best birthday party ever!

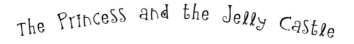

This book belongs to

. . . .

First published in 2018 by Miles Kelly Publishing Ltd
Harding's Barn, Bardfield End Green, Thaxted, Essex, CM6 3PX, UK

2 4 6 8 10 9 7 5 3 1

Publishing Director Belinda Gallagher
Creative Director Jo Cowan
Editorial Director Rosie Neave
Senior Editor Becky Miles
Design Managers Joe Jones, Simon Lee
Image Manager Liberty Newton
Production Elizabeth Collins, Caroline Kelly
Reprographics Stephan Davis, Jennifer Cozens
Assets Lorraine King

ISBN 978-1-78617-482-6

Printed in China

British Library Cataloguing-in-Publication Data
A catalogue record for this book is available from the British Library

Acknowledgements

The publishers would like to thank the following artists who have contributed to this book:
Advocate Art: Natalia Moore
The Bright Agency: Maddie Frost (decorative frames), Clair Rossiter

Made with paper from a sustainable forest

www.mileskelly.net

Earl Mar's Daughter

♥

The girl and the Lion

Miles Kelly

Earl Mar's Daughter

It was a fine summer's day
as Earl Mar's daughter was
walking in the castle gardens.
She looked up and saw a dove
sitting in an oak tree. She said,
"My dear little dove, fly down to

4

me. I will take you home and keep you as my pet." As she spoke, the dove flew onto her shoulder, so she took it home with her.

But as night came Earl Mar's daughter was surprised to find a handsome young man sitting by her bed. "I am that dove you brought home," he said, and he told her that he was really a prince called Florentine, and his

mother had put a spell on him.

"She changed me into a dove by day. But at night her spell loses its power and I am a man again," he said.

The prince said he would love Earl Mar's daughter forever and never leave her side if she married him. So the prince and Earl Mar's daughter were married in secret. They lived happily in the castle and no one

Earl Mar's Daughter

knew that every night the little
white dove changed into Prince
Florentine, and that every year a
little son was born to Earl Mar's
daughter. Prince Florentine flew
over the sea with their baby son
on his back, and
left the baby with
his mother.

   After seven
years Earl Mar
said it was time

his daughter got married. He didn't know that she was already secretly married to Prince Florentine. His daughter said, "Dear father, I don't want to marry. I am happy here with my dove." This made her father angry and he said he would get rid of her dove.

Prince Florentine had to leave the castle quickly. So he flew over the deep, blue sea until he

came to his mother's castle. He asked his mother if she could help, but she said, "I'm sorry, but my magic doesn't reach that far." Instead she told him to go to a more powerful witch called Ostree.

The prince did this, and the powerful witch changed him into a bigger bird. She also sent other large birds to help him.

Prince Florentine and the

Earl Mar's Daughter

flock of birds flew back across the sea to Earl Mar's castle. They arrived just as his daughter was about to be married to someone else. The birds swooped down and picked up Earl Mar's daughter and carried her back to Prince Florentine's mother.

Earl Mar's Daughter

As they all arrived,
the spell was broken
and the prince was
no longer a dove. So
Prince Florentine,
Earl Mar's daughter
and their seven sons lived
happily ever after.

The Girl and the Lion

There was once a poor girl who looked after cows. One morning she was taking her cows through a field when she heard a loud growl. There in the grass she saw a lion sitting holding up

its paw. The girl could see a big
thorn, which looked very painful.
She bravely removed the thorn
and bandaged the lion's paw.

When the girl went back
to her cows they were gone.
She looked
everywhere

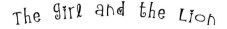

but couldn't find them. Her
master was cross with her for
letting them escape. In their
place he gave her his donkeys
to look after.

Every day the girl took the
donkeys to graze in the woods.
Then one morning, she heard a
growl. She saw the same lion
lying on the ground, this time
with a big cut across his face.
The girl was not at all afraid,

and she rushed over to the lion to wash his cut.

When the girl went back to her donkeys they too had disappeared. She looked for them everywhere but couldn't find them. Her master was even more cross than the last time. This time he gave her his pigs to look after.

The next day she took the pigs out to feed, and the day

after that. On the following day
the girl heard a growl for a
third time. She found her old
friend the lion, with a cut paw,
lying under a tree. The girl
washed and bandaged the paw

to make it better.

Then she went back to her pigs, but just like the cows and the donkeys, the pigs had gone. She climbed a tree to get a better view of the land. Soon night fell, and as she sat in the branches the girl saw something strange. A young man pulled aside a rock from a cave and crept behind it. The girl stayed

17

in the tree
all night. In the
morning, the lion came
out from behind the rock.
She waited until nightfall,
then the man appeared
again. The girl asked him
who he was. The man told her
that he was really a prince, and
that a giant had put a spell on
him. So he was a lion by day
and a prince at night. The girl

asked how she could break
the spell.

"You need to get a lock of
hair from a princess and spin it
into a coat for the giant."

So the girl went to work in
the palace, where she made
sure that her hair always looked
beautiful. The princess noticed
this, and asked the girl to do
her hair too. Every day the girl
combed the princess's hair so

that it shone like the sun. One day the girl dared to ask the princess for a lock of her hair.

"You may have a lock of my hair if you find me a prince to marry," said the princess. So the girl cut off a lock of the

The girl and the Lion

princess's hair and spun it into a glittering coat. Then she climbed a mountain to take the coat to the giant.

She bravely presented the coat to the giant, who was pleased with the gift.

"In return, you may have one wish," the giant said. The girl asked for the spell to be removed from the prince so he was no longer a lion.

21

The Girl and the Lion

The giant said, "To break the spell, you must make the lion swim in a magic lake that lies over the mountains, far away."

The girl returned to the prince and told him what the giant had said. She was scared it was a trick and didn't want to the lion to be hurt.

"I will do it," the prince told her. So the girl and the lion walked for two days until they came to the lake. The lion was frightened of water but he bravely dived in.

Then, all of a sudden, out of the lake walked the prince, as handsome as could be! He

thanked the girl for saving him and asked her to marry him. But she wept, and told him of her promise to the princess. So they went to the palace to see the princess. When the princess saw the prince she was so happy, as he was her long-lost brother.

The prince and the girl were married, so she became a princess, and they lived happily ever after.